Sharon Kendr[ick] [...] competition, desc[...] an exotic island b[...] did she realise tha[...] job! Today she wr[...] Mills & Boon, featuring her often stubborn but always *to-die-for* heroes and the women who bring them to their knees. She believes that the best books are those you never want to end. Just like life…

Maisey Yates is a *USA Today* bestselling author of more than thirty romance novels. She has a coffee habit she has no interest in kicking, and a slight Pinterest addiction. She lives with her husband and children in the Pacific Northwest. When Maisey isn't writing she can be found singing in the grocery store, shopping for shoes online, and probably not doing dishes. Check out her website: www.maiseyyates.com.

Michelle Smart's love affair with books started when she was a baby, when she would cuddle them in her cot. A voracious reader of all genres, she found her love of romance established when she stumbled across her first Mills & Boon book at the age of twelve. She's been reading (and writing) them ever since. Michelle lives in Northamptonshire, with her husband and two young Smarties.

His Christmas Conquest

SHARON KENDRICK

MAISEY YATES

MICHELLE SMART

MILLS & BOON

First Published in Great Britain 2018
By Mills & Boon, an imprint of HarperCollins *Publishers*
1 London Bridge Street, London, SE1 9GF

HIS CHRISTMAS CONQUEST © 2018 Harlequin Books S.A.

The Sheikh's Christmas Conquest © 2015 Sharon Kendrick
A Christmas Vow of Seduction © 2015 Maisey Yates
Claiming His Christmas Consequence © 2016 Michelle Smart

ISBN: 978-0-263-26841-6

1018

MIX
Paper from
responsible sources
FSC™ C007454

This book is produced from independently certified FSC™ paper to ensure responsible forest management.

For more information visit: www.harpercollins.co.uk/green

Printed and bound in Spain
by CPI, Barcelona

THE SHEIKH'S
CHRISTMAS
CONQUEST

SHARON KENDRICK

To the amazing Anni MacDonald-Hall – who taught me SO MUCH about horses. Sheikh Saladin Al Mektala is very grateful for her expertise

CHAPTER ONE

LIVVY WAS HANGING mistletoe when the doorbell rang. Expensive, mocking mistletoe tied with ribbon the colour of blood. The sudden sound startled her because the heavy snow had made the world silent and she wasn't expecting anyone until Christmas Eve.

Go away, whoever you are, she thought as several white berries bounced onto the floor like miniature ping-pong balls. But the doorbell rang again—for much longer this time—because whoever was outside had decided to jam their thumb against the buzzer.

Livvy wished the unwanted caller would vanish, because there was still so much to do before the guests arrived, and the snowfall meant that Stella, her part-time help, hadn't turned up. But you couldn't run a successful business and behave like a prima donna—even if it was only four days before Christmas and you didn't have any room vacancies. She climbed down the ladder with a feeling of irritation that died the instant she opened the door.

She was unprepared for the man who stood on her doorstep. A stranger, yet not quite a stranger—although it took a moment for her to place him. He was famous in the horse-racing world she'd once inhabited. Some might say infamous. He was certainly unforgettable with eyes like gleaming jet and rich olive skin that showcased his hawklike features. His hard body spoke of exercise and discipline, and he was the kind of man who would make you take a second glance and then maybe a third.

But it wasn't just his appearance or his undeniable charisma that made Livvy blink her eyes in disbelief—it was his lofty status. Because it wasn't just any man who stood there surveying her so unsmilingly—it was Saladin Al Mektala, the king of Jazratan. A real-life desert sheikh standing on *her* doorstep.

She wondered if there was some sort of protocol for greeting one of the world's wealthiest men, especially when they also happened to be royal. Once upon a time she might have been intimidated by his reputation and his presence—but not anymore. She'd had to do a lot of growing up these past few years and her experiences had made her strong. These days she lived an independent life she was proud of—even if currently it felt as if she was clinging on to that independence by her fingernails.

'Didn't anyone ever tell you,' she said, tipping her head to one side, 'that it's polite to wait for someone to answer the first ring, rather than deafening them with a repeated summons?'

Saladin raised his eyebrows, unable to hide his surprise at her feisty response. It was an untraditional greeting to receive, even here in England where the demands of protocol were less rigid than in his homeland. But even so. His royal presence was usually enough to guarantee total deference, and although he sometimes complained to his advisors that people were never *normal* around him, he missed deference when it wasn't there.

He narrowed his eyes and studied her. 'Do you know who I am?'

She laughed. She actually laughed—her shiny ponytail swaying from side to side, like the tail of a chestnut horse.

'I thought that was the kind of question B-list celebrities asked when they were trying to get into the latest seedy nightclub,' she said.

Saladin felt a flicker of annoyance and something else. Something that was a little harder to define. He had been warned that she was difficult. That she could be prickly and stubborn—but these were qualities that were usually melted away by the sheer force of his personality and his position in society. And, not to put too fine a point on it, by his impact on the opposite sex, who usually melted like ice in the desert whenever he was around. His instinct was to bite back a withering response to put her in her place, but Livvy Miller had something he badly wanted so that he was forced to adopt a reasonable tone, something that didn't come easily to him. 'It was a genuine question,' he said. 'I am Saladin Al Mektala.'

'I know who you are.'

'And my office have been trying to contact you.' He paused. 'Repeatedly.'

She smiled, but Saladin noted that the smile did not reach her eyes.

'I know that, too,' she said. 'In fact, they've been bombarding me with emails and phone calls for the past week. I've barely been able to switch on my computer without a new message from palace@jazratan.com pinging into my inbox.'

'Yet you chose to ignore them?'

'That is my prerogative, surely?' She leaned on the doorjamb, her unusual eyes shaded by their forest of lashes. 'I gave them the same answer every time. I told them I wasn't interested. If they were unable to accept that, then surely the fault lies with them. My position hasn't changed.'

Saladin could barely disguise his growing irritation. 'But you don't know what it is they were asking of you.'

'Something to do with a horse. And that was enough for me.'

She drew herself up to her full height but he still towered over her. He found himself thinking that he could probably lift her up with one hand. When he'd heard about her ability to soothe huge and very temperamental horses, he'd never imagined she could be so...petite.

'Because I don't have anything to do with horses anymore,' she finished gravely.

Dragging his gaze from her slender frame to eyes that were the colour of honey, he fixed her with a questioning look. 'Why not?'

She gave a little clicking sound of irritation, but not before he had seen something dark in her eyes. A flash of something uncomfortable that he stored away for future reference.

'That's really none of your business,' she said, tilting her chin in a gesture of defiance. 'I don't have to offer any kind of explanation for my decisions, particularly to people who turn up unannounced on my doorstep at one of the busiest times of the year.'

Saladin felt the first flicker of heat. And of challenge. He was not used to resistance, or defiance. In his world, whatever he wanted was his. A click of his fingers or a cool glance was usually enough to guarantee him whatever he desired. Certainly, this kind of opposition was largely unknown to him, and certainly when it came from a woman, because women enjoyed submitting to his will—not opposing it. His response was one of renewed determination, which was quickly followed by the first sweet shimmer of sexual arousal and that surprised him. Because although Olivia Miller was reputed to have a magical touch when it came to horses, she certainly hadn't applied the same fairy dust to her appearance.

Saladin's lips curled. She was one of those women who the English called tomboys—and he didn't approve, for weren't women supposed to look like women? Her hair was pale brown, touched by red—a colour named after the great Italian painter Titian and a colour rare enough to be admired—but it was tied back in a functional ponytail, and her freckled face was completely bare of artifice. Why, even her jeans failed to do the only commendable thing that jeans were capable of—they were loose around her bottom instead of clinging to it like syrup. Which made the undeniable stir of lust he was feeling difficult to understand. Because why on earth should he be attracted to someone who sublimated her femininity as much as possible?

He narrowed his eyes. 'Are you aware that your attitude could be termed as insolence?' he questioned softly. 'And that it is unwise to answer the king of Jazratan in such a way?'

Again, that defiant tilt of the chin. He wondered if

she was aware that such a positioning of her face made her look as if she were inviting him to kiss her.

'I wasn't intending to be insolent,' she said, although the message in her eyes told him otherwise. 'I was simply stating a fact. What I chose to do with my life has nothing to do with you. I owe you no explanation. I am not one of your royal subjects.'

'No, you are not, but you might at least grant me the courtesy of hearing what I have to say,' he bit out. 'Or does the word *hospitality* mean nothing to you? Are you aware that I have travelled many miles in the most inclement weather in order to meet you?'

Livvy eyed the remaining bunches of mistletoe still waiting to be hung and thought about all the other things that needed to be done before her guests arrived. She wanted to make more cake to fill the house with sweet smells, and there were fires to make up in all the bedrooms. Her to-do list was as long as her arm and this handsome and vaguely intimidating stranger was hindering her. 'You could have chosen a more convenient time than just before Christmas,' she said.

'And when would have been a more *convenient* time?' he retorted. 'When you have consistently refused to be pinned down?'

'Most people would have taken the hint and cut their losses.'

'I am a king. I don't do *hints*' came his stony response.

Livvy hesitated. His behaviour confirmed everything she'd ever heard about him. He had been known for his arrogance on the racing circuit—seemingly with good reason—and she was so tempted to tell him to go. But she *was* running a business—even if it was currently a struggling business—and if she angered Saladin Al Mektala any more than he was already clearly angered, he might just spread a malicious word or two around the place. She could imagine it would be easy for someone like him to drip a little more poison onto her already damaged reputation. And adverse publicity could be death if you worked in the hospitality industry.

Behind him, she could see the falling snow, which had been coming down in bucketloads since before breakfast. Fat flakes were tumbling past like a never-ending slide show. Lawns that earlier had been merely spattered with the stuff now sported a thick white mantle—as if someone had been layering on cotton wool while she hadn't been looking. If it carried on like this, the lanes would soon be impassable and she'd never get rid of him. And she wanted to get rid of him. She didn't like him dominating her doorway and ex-uding all that *testosterone* and making her think about stuff she hadn't thought about in a long time. *She didn't like the way he made her feel.*

Farther up the drive stood a black four-wheel drive and she wondered if anyone was sitting shivering in-side.

'What about your bodyguards—are they in the car?' Her gaze swept around the wintry garden. 'Hiding in the bushes, perhaps—or waiting to jump from a tree?'

'I don't have any bodyguards with me.'

So they were all alone.

Livvy's anxiety increased. Something about his powerful body and brooding features was making her skin prickle with a weird kind of foreboding—and an even more alarming sense of anticipation. For the first time she found herself wishing that she had a dog who would bark at him, rather than a soppy feline mop called Peppa, who was currently stretched out in front of the fire in the drawing room, purring happily.

But she wasn't going to allow this man to intimidate her. And if she wasn't intimidated, then it followed that she shouldn't keep avoiding a meeting with him. Maybe this was the only way he would understand that she meant what she said. If she kept repeating that she wasn't interested in whatever he was offering, then surely he would have no choice other than to believe her. And to leave her alone.

'You'd better come in,' she said as an icy gust brought a flurry of snow into the hall. 'I can give you thirty minutes but no longer. I'm expecting guests for Christmas and I have a lot to do before they arrive.'

She saw his faintly triumphant smile as he stepped inside and noticed how the elegant proportions of the airy entrance hall seemed to shrink once she had closed the front door on the snowy afternoon. There was something so intensely *masculine* about him, she thought reluctantly. Something that was both exciting and dangerous—and she forced herself to take a deep breath in an attempt to slow the sudden galloping of her heart. *Act as if he's a guest*, she told herself. *Put on your best, bright smile and switch on your professional hospitality mode.*

'Why don't you come into the drawing room?' she suggested politely. 'There's a fire there.'

He nodded and she saw his narrowed gaze take in the high ceilings and the elaborate wooden staircase as he followed her across the hallway. 'This is a beautiful old house,' he observed, a note of approval deepening his voice.

'Thank you,' she said, automatically slipping into

her role as guide. 'Parts of it date back to the twelfth century. They certainly don't build them like this anymore—perhaps that's a good thing, considering the amount of maintenance that's needed.' The building's history was one of the reasons why people travelled to this out-of-the-way spot to hire a room. Because the past defined the present and people hungered after the idea of an elegant past. Or at least, they had—until the rise of several nearby boutique hotels had started offering the kind of competition that was seriously affecting her turnover.

But Livvy couldn't deny her thrill of pleasure as the sheikh walked into the drawing room, because she was proud of her old family home, despite the fact that it had started to look a little frayed around the edges.

The big fire was banked with apple logs, which scented the air, and although the huge Christmas tree was still bare there weren't many rooms that could accommodate a tree of that size. At some point later she would have to drag herself up to the dusty attic and haul down the decorations, which had been in the family since the year dot, and go through the ritual of bringing the tree to life. Soon it would be covered in spangles and fairy lights and topped with the ancient little angel she'd once made with her mother. And for a while, Christmas would work its brief and sometimes unbearable magic of merging past and present.

She looked up to find Saladin Al Mektala studying her intently and, once again, a shiver of something inexplicable made her nostalgic sentiments dissolve as she began to study him right back.

He wasn't dressed like a sheikh. There were no flowing robes or billowing headdress to indicate his desert king status. The dark cashmere overcoat that he was removing—without having been invited to—was worn over dark trousers and a charcoal sweater that hugged his honed torso. He looked disturbingly *modern*, she thought—even if the flinty glint of his dark eyes made him seem disturbingly primitive. She watched as he hung the cashmere coat over the back of a chair and saw the gleam of melted snow on his black hair as he stepped a little closer to the fire.

'So,' she said. 'You must want something very badly if you're prepared to travel to the wilds of Derbyshire in order to get it.'

'Oh, but I do,' he said silkily. 'I want you.'

Something in his sultry tone kick-started feelings Livvy had repressed for longer than she cared to remember and for a split second, she found herself imagining what it would feel like to be the object of desire to a man like Saladin Al Mektala. Would those flinty eyes soften before he kissed you? Would a woman feel *helpless* if she was being held in arms as powerful as his?

She swallowed, surprised by the unexpected path her thoughts had taken her down because she didn't fall in lust with total strangers. Actually, she didn't fall in lust at all. She quickly justified her wayward fantasy by reminding herself that he was being deliberately provocative and had made that statement in such a way—as if he was *seeking* to shock her. 'You'll have to be a little more specific than that,' she said crisply. 'What do you want me to do?'

His face changed as the provocation left it and she saw a shadow pass over the hawklike features. 'I have a sick horse,' he said, his voice tightening. 'A badly injured stallion. My favourite.'

His distress affected her—how could it fail to do so? But Livvy hardened her heart to his problems, because didn't she have enough of her own? 'I'm sorry to hear that,' she said. 'But as a king of considerable wealth, no doubt you have the best veterinary surgeons at your disposal. I'm sure they'll be able to work out some plan of action for your injured horse.'

'They say not.'

'Really?' Linking her fingers together, she looked up at him. 'What exactly is the problem?'

'A suspensory ligament,' he said, 'which has torn away from the bone.'

Livvy winced. 'That's bad.'

'I know it's bad,' he gritted out. 'Why the hell do you think I'm here?'

She decided to ignore his rudeness. 'There are revolutionary new treatments out there today,' she said placatingly. 'You can inject stem cells, or you could try shockwave treatment. I've heard that's very good.'

'You think I haven't already tried everything? That I haven't flown out every equine expert to examine him?' he demanded. 'And yet everything has failed. The finest specialists in the world have pronounced themselves at a loss.' There was a pause as he swallowed and his voice became dark and distorted as he spoke. 'They have told me there is no hope.'

For a moment, Livvy felt a deep sense of pity because she knew how powerful the bond between a man and his horse could be—especially a man whose exalted position meant that he could probably put more trust in animals than in humans. But she also knew that sometimes you had to accept things as they were and not as you wanted them to be. That you couldn't defeat nature, no matter how much you tried. And that all the money in the world would make no difference to the outcome.

She saw the steely glint in his dark eyes as he looked at her and recognised it as the look of someone who wasn't intending to give up. Was this what being a king did to a man—made you believe you could shape the world to your own wishes? She sighed. 'Like I said, I'm very sorry to hear that. But if you've been told there's no hope, then I don't know how you expect me to help.'

'Yes, you do, Livvy,' he said forcefully. 'You know you do.'

His fervent words challenged her nearly as much as his sudden use of his name.

'No. I don't.' She shook her head. 'I don't have anything to do with horses anymore. I haven't done for years. That part of my life is over, and if anyone has told you anything different, then they're wrong. I'm sorry.'

There was a pause. 'May I sit down?'

His words startled her as he indicated one of the faded brocade chairs that sat beside the blazing fire—and his sudden change of tactic took her by surprise. And not just surprise. Because if she was being honest, wasn't there something awfully flattering about a sheikh asking if he could prolong his stay and sit down? Briefly, she wondered if he would let her use his endorsement on her website. 'The Sheikh of Jazratan loves to relax in front of the old-fashioned fire.' She met the cold glitter of his eyes. Probably not.

'If you want,' she said as she turned on one of the

lamps so that the fading afternoon was lit with something other than firelight.

But her heart began to race as he sat down—because it seemed disturbingly intimate to see his muscular body unfold into a chair that suddenly looked insubstantial, and for those endlessly long legs to stretch out in front of him. He looked like a panther who had taken an uncharacteristic moment of relaxation, who had wandered in from the wild into a domestic domain, but all the time you were aware that beneath the sheathed paws lay deadly claws. Was that why her cat suddenly opened its eyes and hissed at him, before jumping up and stalking from the room with her tail held high? Too late she realised she should have said no. She should have made him realise she meant what she said before ejecting him into the snowy afternoon before the light faded.

'So,' she said, with a quick glance at her watch. 'Like I said, I have things I need to do, so maybe you could just cut to the chase?'

'An ironic choice of words in the circumstances,' he commented drily. 'Or perhaps deliberate? Either way, it is unlikely that my stallion will race again, even though he has won nearly every major prize in the racing calendar. In fact, he is in so much pain that the vets have told me that it is cruel to let him continue like this and…' His voice tailed off.

'And?'

He leaned his head back against the chair and his eyes narrowed—dark shards that glinted in the firelight. 'And you have a gift with horses, Livvy,' he said softly. 'A rare gift. You can heal them.'

'Who told you that?

'My trainer. He described to me a woman who was the best horsewoman he'd ever seen. He said that she was as light as a feather but strong as an ox—but that her real skill lay in her interaction with the animal. He said that the angriest horse in the stables would grow calm whenever she grew close. He said he'd seen her do stuff with horses that defied logic, and astounded all the horse vets.' His voice deepened as his dark eyes grew watchful. 'And that they used to call you the horse whisperer.'

It was a long time since Livvy had heard the phrase that had once followed her around like mud on a rainy day at the stables. A phrase that carried its own kind of mystique and made people believe she was some kind of witch. And she wasn't. She was just an ordinary person who wanted to be left to get on with her life.

She bent to pick up a log so that her face was hidden, and by the time she straightened up she had composed herself enough to face his inquisitive stare and to answer him in a steady voice.

'That's all hocus-pocus,' she said. 'Nothing but an old wives' tale and people believing what they want to believe. I just got lucky, that's all. The law of probability says that the horses I helped "heal" would have got better on their own anyway.'

'But I know that sometimes nature can contradict the laws of probability,' he contradicted softly. 'Didn't one of your most famous poets say something on those lines?'

'I don't read poetry,' she said flatly.

'Maybe you should.'

Her smile was tight. 'Just like I don't take advice from strangers.'

His eyes glittered. 'Then, come and work for me and we'll be strangers no longer.'

With a jerky movement she threw another log onto the grate and it sparked into life with a whoosh of flames. Had he deliberately decided to use charm—knowing how effective it could be on someone who was awkward around men? She knew about his reputation but, even if she hadn't, you needed only to look at him to realise that he could have a woman eating out of his hand as easily as you could get a stroppy horse to munch on a sugar cube.

'Look,' she said, trying to sound less abrasive, because he was probably one of those men who responded best to a woman when she was cooing at him. 'I'm sorry I can't help you, but I haven't got a magic wand I can wave to make your horse better. And although I'm obviously flattered that you should have thought of me, I'm just not interested in your offer.'

Saladin felt a flicker of frustration. She didn't sound flattered at all. What was the matter with her? Didn't she realise that accepting this job would carry a huge financial reward—not to mention the kudos of being employed by the royal house of Al Mektala?

He had done his research. He knew that this ancient house she'd inherited was written up in all the guidebooks as somewhere worth visiting and that she ran it as some kind of bed and breakfast business. But the place was going to rack and ruin—anyone could see that. Old houses like this drank money as greedily as the desert sands soaked up water, and it was clear to him that she didn't have a lot of cash to splash about. The brocade chair on which he sat had a spring that was sticking into his buttocks, and the walls beside the fireplace could have done with a coat of paint. His eyes narrowed. Couldn't she see he was offering her the opportunity to earn the kind of sum that would enable her to give the place a complete facelift?

And what about her, with her tomboy clothes and freckled face? She had turned her back on the riding world that had once been her life. She had hidden herself away in the middle of nowhere, serving up cooked breakfasts to the random punters who came to stay. What kind of a life was that for a woman who was nearly thirty? In his own country, a woman was married with at least two children by the age of twenty-five, because it was the custom to marry young. He thought of Alya and a spear of pain lanced through his heart. He remembered dreams crushed and the heavy sense of blame, and he cursed the nature of his thoughts and pushed them away as he looked into Olivia Miller's stubborn face.

'You might not have a magic wand, but I would like you to try. What is it that you say? Nothing ventured, nothing gained. And I think you will discover that the financial rewards I'm offering will be beyond your wildest dreams.' He tilted the corners of his mouth in a brief smile. 'And surely you don't want to look a gift horse in the mouth?'

She didn't respond to his attempt at humour, she just continued to stare at him, only now there was a distinct flicker of annoyance in her amber eyes. Saladin felt another rush of sexual attraction, because women didn't often glare at him like that and he was finding her truculence a surprising turn-on. Because no woman had ever refused him anything.

'How many ways do I have to say no before you'll believe I mean it?' she said.

'And how long will it take you to realise that I am a very persistent man who is used to getting what I want?'

'Persist away—you won't change my mind.'

And suddenly Saladin did what he'd told himself he was only going to do as a last resort, which he seemed now to have reached. He leaned back, his eyes not leaving her face. 'So is this how you are intending to spend the rest of your life, Livvy?' he questioned softly. 'Hiding yourself away in the middle of nowhere and neglecting a talent that few possess—and all because some man once left you standing at the altar?'

CHAPTER TWO

At first Livvy didn't react to Saladin's cruel taunt because not reacting was something she was good at. One of the things she'd taught herself to do when the man she'd been due to marry had decided not to bother turning up. She'd learned not to show what she was feeling. Not to give the watching world any idea what was going on inside her head, or her heart. But the sheikh's words hurt. Even now, they hurt. Even though it was a long time since anybody had been crass enough to remind her that she had once been *jilted*. That she had stood at the altar wearing a stupid white dress and an eager smile, which had faded as the minutes had ticked by and the silence had grown into hushed and increasingly urgent whispers as it had dawned on the waiting congregation that the groom wasn't going to show.

She looked at the man sitting there with firelight illuminating his hawklike face and in that moment she actually *hated* him. How dare he bring up something so painful just so he could get what *he* wanted? Didn't he care about hurting people's feelings and trampling all over them—or was he simply a master of manipulation? Didn't he realise that such a public humiliation had dealt her self-confidence a blow from which it had taken a long time to recover? And maybe it had never completely recovered. It had still been powerful enough to make her want to leave her old life behind and start a new one. To leave the horses she'd once adored and to view all subsequent advances from men with suspicion.

She would like to take a run at him and *shake* him. To batter her fists against that hard, broad chest and tell him that he was an uncaring beast. But she suspected her rage would be wasted on such a powerful man, and mightn't he regard such a strong response as some petty kind of victory?

'My abandoned marriage has nothing to do with my reasons for not wanting to work for you,' she said, with a coolness she'd cultivated to cope with all the questions she'd had to deal with afterwards. And she'd needed it. She remembered the badly disguised glee in the voices of the women—those wafer-thin blondes who couldn't understand why Rupert de Vries had proposed to someone as unremarkable as her in the first place. *He didn't say why? You mean you honestly had no idea?* No. She'd honestly had no idea. What woman would ever subject herself to that kind of public ridicule if she'd had any inkling the groom was going to do a runner?

She glared into Saladin's glittering dark eyes. 'Though the fact that you even asked the question is another mark against you.'

His dark brows knitted together. 'What are you talking about?'

'I'm talking about the fact that you've obviously been delving into my private life, which isn't making me feel very favourable towards you. No person likes to feel they're being spied on, and you're not doing a very good job of selling yourself as a prospective employer.'

'I don't usually have to sell myself,' he replied, with a coolness that matched hers. 'And surely you can understand why I always investigate people I'm planning to employ.'

'When are you going to accept that you won't be employing me?'

He opened his mouth and then shut it, turning to look around the room, his gaze coming to rest on the faded velvet curtains, as if he'd only just noticed that the sun had bleached them and that moths had been attacking some of the lining.

Had he noticed?

'So is your bed and breakfast business thriving?' he questioned casually.

It was quite clear what he was getting at and suddenly Livvy wanted to prove him wrong. So just *show him*, she thought—though it didn't occur to her until afterwards that she wasn't obliged to show him anything. She wondered if it was pride that made her want to elevate her image from jilted bride to that of budding entrepreneur, even though it wasn't exactly true.

'Indeed it is. It's been a very popular destination,' she said. 'Historic houses like this have a wide appeal to the general public and people can't get enough of them. Speaking of which…' Pointedly, she looked at her watch. 'Your half hour is almost up.'

'But it must be hard work?' he persisted.

She met the mocking question in his black eyes. 'Of course it is. Cooking up to eight different breakfasts to order and making up beds with clean linen most days is not for the faint-hearted. But I've never been afraid of hard work. You don't get anything for nothing in this life.' She paused, her smile growing tight. 'Although I suppose someone like you might be the exception to the rule.'

Not showing any sign of moving, he surveyed her steadily. 'And why might that be?'

'Well, you're a sheikh, aren't you?' she said. 'You're one of the richest men in the world. You own a string of prizewinning racehorses and a palace—for all I know, you might own hundreds of palaces. You have your own plane, I imagine.'

'And?'

'And you've probably never had to lift a finger to acquire the kind of wealth you take for granted. You've probably had everything handed to you on a plate.'

There was silence as Saladin felt a flicker of exasperation. It was an accusation levelled at most people born to royal status, but never usually voiced in his presence because usually people didn't dare. Yes, he was unimaginably rich—but did she think that he had grown up in a bubble? That he'd never had to fight for his country and his people? That he'd never known heartbreak, or stared into the dark abyss of real loss? Once again, Alya's beautiful and perfect face swam into his memory, but he pushed it aside as he met the Englishwoman's quizzical gaze.

'Materially I do not deny that I have plenty,' he said. 'But what about you? You're not exactly on the breadline, are you, Livvy? This place is hardly your average house. You, too, have known privilege.'

Livvy wished he would move away from her, because his presence was making her feel distinctly uncomfortable. As if her plaid shirt had suddenly become too small and her breasts were straining against the tightening buttons. As if those watchful eyes could somehow see through her clothes to the plain and functional underwear that lay beneath.

'It's a rare Georgian house,' she agreed, her fingers playing with the top button of her shirt. 'And I'm lucky to live here. It's been in my family for many years.'

'But the maintenance costs must be high,' he mused.

'Astronomical,' she agreed. 'Which is why I open the house to paying guests.'

He was glancing up at the ceiling now. Had he noticed the ugly damp stain then, or did the firelight successfully hide it? His gaze was lowered and redirected to her face, where once again it seemed to burn its way over her skin.

'So how's business, Livvy—generally?'

Her smile was bland. 'Business is good.'

'Your guests don't mind the fact that the paint is peeling, or that the plaster is crumbling on that far wall?'

'I doubt it. People come looking for history, not pristine paintwork—you can find that almost anywhere in some of the cheaper hotel chains.'

'You know, I could offer you a lot of money,' he observed, after a moment or two. 'Enough to pay for the kind of work this place is crying out for. I could throw in a little extra if you like—so that you could afford the holiday you look as if you need.'

Livvy stiffened. Was he implying that she looked washed out? Almost without her thinking, her fingers crept up to her hairline to brush away a stray strand that must have escaped from her ponytail. It was true she hadn't had a holiday in ages. And it was also true that her debts continued to grow, no matter how many new bookings she took. Sometimes she felt like Canute trying to turn back the tide, and now she couldn't remember how Canute had actually coped. Had he just admitted defeat and given up?

She wished Saladin would stop looking at her like that—his black eyes capturing her in their dark and hypnotic spotlight. She wasn't a vain woman by any definition of the word, but she would have taken a bit more trouble with her appearance if she'd known that a desert sheikh was going to come calling. Suddenly her scalp felt itchy and her face hot, and her shirt still felt as if it had shrunk in the wash.

'Is that your answer to everything?' she questioned. 'To write a cheque and to hell with anything else?'

He shrugged. 'Why wouldn't it be—when I have the capability to do exactly that, and money talks louder than anything else?'

'You cynic,' she breathed.

'I'm not denying that.' He gave a soft laugh. 'Or maybe you're just naive. Money talks, Livvy—it talks louder than anything else. It's about the only thing in life you can rely on—which is why you should do yourself a favour and come with me to Jazratan. My stable complex is the finest in the world and it would be interesting for you to see it.'

He smiled at her, but Livvy sensed it was a calculating smile. As if he had only produced it because it would add a touch of lightness to conversation that wasn't going the way he intended.

'Come and work with my horse and I'll give you whatever you want, within reason,' he continued. 'And if you cure Burkaan—if you ensure that a gun will not be held to his head while I am forced to stare into his trusting and bewildered eyes as the life bleeds out of him, you will walk away knowing that you need never worry about money again.'

The heartfelt bit about the horse got to her much more than the financial incentive he was offering. In fact, she hated the mercenary progression of his words. As if everything had a price—even people. As if you could wear them down just by increasing the amount of money on the table. Maybe in his world, that was what happened.

But despite her determination not to be tempted, she *was* tempted. For a minute she allowed herself to think what she could do with the money. Where would she even start? By tackling the ancient wiring in some of the bedrooms, or sorting out the antiquated boiler that badly needed replacing? She thought about the icy corridors upstairs and the lack of insulation in the roof. Most of the heat was pumped into the guest bed-rooms, leaving her own windows coated with a thin layer of ice each morning. She shivered. It had been a bitter winter and they were still only a third of the way through it, and she was getting fed up with having to wear thick socks to bed at night.

'I can't,' she said. 'I have guests who are due to spend the holidays here who are arriving in a couple of days. I can't just cancel their Christmas and New Year when they've spent months looking forward to it. You'll just have to find someone else.'

Saladin's mouth tightened, but still he wasn't done. Didn't she realise that he would get what he wanted in the end, no matter how he had to go about it? That if it came to a battle of wills, he would win. Spurred on by the almost imperceptible note of hesitation he'd heard in her voice, he got up from his chair and walked over to the window. It was almost dark, but the heavy clouds had already leached the sky of all colour and all you could see was snow. It had highlighted all the leafless trees with ghostly white fingers. It had blanketed his parked car so that all that was visible was a snowy mound.

His eyes narrowed as fat flakes swirled down, transformed into tumbling gold feathers by the light streaming from the window. He ran through the possibilities of what he should do next, knowing his choices were limited. He could go and get his car started before the snow came down any harder. He could drive off and come back again tomorrow. Give her time to think about his offer and realise that she would be a fool to reject it. Or he could have his people deal with it, using rather more ruthless back-room tactics.

He turned back to see her unsmiling face and he was irritated by his inability to get through to her. Logic told him to leave, yet for some reason he was reluctant to do so, even though she had started walking towards the door, making it clear that she expected him to trail after her. A woman who wanted him gone? Unbelievable! When had any woman ever turned him away?

He followed her out into the wood-lined corridor, which was lit by lamps on either side, realising that she was close enough to touch. And bizarrely, he thought about kissing her. About claiming those stubborn and unpainted lips with his own and waiting to see how long it would take before she was breathlessly agreeing to anything he asked of her.

But his choices were suddenly taken away from him by a dramatic intervention as the lights went out and the corridor was plunged into darkness. From just ahead of him, he heard Livvy gasp and then he felt the softness of her body as she stumbled back against him.

CHAPTER THREE

As the corridor was plunged into darkness, Saladin's hands automatically reached out to steady the stumbling Livvy. At least, that was what he told himself. He thought afterwards that if she'd been a man he wouldn't have let his hands linger on her for quite so long, nor his fingers to grip her slender body quite so tightly. But Livvy Miller was a woman—and it had been a long time since he had touched a woman. It had recently been the anniversary of Alya's death and he always shied away from intimacy on either side of that grim date, when pain and loss and regret overwhelmed him. Because to do so felt like a betrayal of his wife's memory—a mechanical act that seemed like a pale version of the real thing. With other women it was just sex—something a man needed in order to function properly. A basic appetite to be fed—and nothing more. But with Alya it had been different. Something that had captured his heart as well as his body.

But maybe for now a body would do...

He felt himself tense with that first, sweet contact—that first touch that set your hormones firing, whether you wanted them to or not. He could feel Livvy's heart beating hard as his hands curved around her ribcage.

The soapy scent that perfumed her skin was both innocent and beguiling, and the tension inside him increased. He found himself wishing he could magic away their clothing and seek relief from the sudden unbearable aching deep inside him. An anonymous coupling in this darkened corridor would be perfect for his needs. It might even have the added benefit of making the stubborn Englishwoman reconsider his offer, because a sexually satisfied woman automatically became a compliant woman.

For a moment he felt her relax against him and he sensed her welcoming softness—as if a split second more would be all the time he needed for her to open up to him. But then she pulled away. Actually, she *snatched* herself away. In the darkness he could hear her struggling to control her breathing and, although he couldn't see the expression on her face, he could hear the panic in her voice.

'What's happened?' she gasped.

It interested him that she'd chosen to ignore that brief but undeniable embrace. He wondered what she would say if he answered truthfully. *I am big enough to explode and I want to put myself inside you and spill my seed.* In his fantasy he knew exactly what he would like her response to be. She would nod and then tear at his clothing with impatient fingers while he dealt swiftly with hers. No need even to undress. Access was all that was required. He would press her up against that wood panelling, and then slide his fingers between her legs while he freed himself. He would kiss her until she was begging him for more, and then he would guide himself to where she was wet and ready, and push deep inside her. It would be quick and it would be meaningless, but he doubted there would be any objections from her.

She was flicking a light switch on and off, but nothing was happening. 'What's happened?' she repeated, only now her voice sounded accusatory.

With a monumental effort he severed his erotic fantasy and let it drift away, concentrating instead on the dense darkness that surrounded them, but his mouth was so dry and his groin so hard that it was several seconds before he was able to answer her question.

'There's been a power cut,' he said.

'I know that,' she howled illogically. 'But how did it happen?'

'I have no idea,' he answered steadily. 'And the how isn't important. We have to deal with it. Do you have your own emergency generator?'

'Are you insane?' Her panicked question came shooting at him through the darkness. 'Of course I don't!'

'Well, then,' he said impatiently. 'Where do you keep your candles?'

Livvy couldn't think straight. He might as well have asked her where the planet Jupiter was in the night sky. Because the sudden loss of light and heating were eclipsed by the realisation that she had been on the brink of losing control. She'd nearly gone to pieces in his arms, because his touch had felt dangerous. And inviting. It had only been the briefest of embraces, but it had been mind-blowing. She hadn't imagined feeling the unmistakable power of his arousal pressing firmly against her. And the amazing thing was that it hadn't shocked her. On the contrary—she'd wanted him to carry on holding her like that. Hadn't she been tempted to turn around and stretch up on tiptoe, to see whether he would kiss her as she sensed he had wanted to? And then to carry on kissing her.

'Candles?' he prompted impatiently.

She swallowed. 'They're…in the kitchen,' she said. 'I'll get them.'

'I'll come with you.'

'You don't think I'm capable of finding my way around my own house?'

'It's dark,' he ground out. 'And we're sticking together.'

Saladin caught hold of her wrist and closed his fingers over it, thinking that if only he had been accompanied by his usual bodyguards and envoys, then someone would now be attempting to fix whatever the problem was.

But he had undertaken this journey alone—instinct telling him that he would have a better chance of success with the Englishwoman without all the dazzle of royal life that inevitably accompanied him. Because some people were intimidated by all the trappings that surrounded a royal sheikh—and, in truth, he liked to shrug off those trappings whenever possible.

When travelling in Europe or the United States, he sometimes got his envoy Zane to act as a decoy sheikh. The two men were remarkably similar in appearance and they had long ago discovered that one powerful robed figure wearing a headdress in the back of a speeding car was interchangeable with another, to all but the most perceptive eye.

In Jazratan he sometimes took solo trips deep into the heart of the desert. At other times he had been known to dress as a merchant and to blend into the thronging crowds of the marketplace in the capital city of Janubwardi. It gave him a certain kick to listen to what his people were saying about him when they thought they were free to do so. His advisors didn't like it, but that was tough. He refused to be treated with kid gloves, especially here in England—a country he knew well. And he knew that the dangers in life were the ones where obvious risk was involved, but the ones that hit you totally out of the blue…

He could feel her pulse slamming wildly beneath his fingers.

'Let me go,' she whispered.

'No. You're not going anywhere,' he snapped. 'Stick close to me—I'm going first. And be careful.'

'I don't need you to tell me to be careful. Don't you have a phone? We could use it as a torch instead of stumbling around in the dark.'

'It's in my car,' he said as they edged along a corridor that seemed less dense now that his eyes had started to accustom themselves to the lack of light. 'Where's yours?'

'In my bedroom.'

'Handy,' he said sarcastically.

'I wasn't expecting to be marooned in the darkness with a total stranger.'

'Spare me the melodrama, Livvy. And let's just concentrate on getting there without falling over.'

Cautiously, they moved along the ancient passage. The flagged floors echoed as she led him down a narrow flight of stairs, into a large windowless kitchen that was as dark as pitch. She wriggled her hand free and felt her way towards a cupboard, where he could hear her scrabbling around—before uttering a little cry of triumph as she located the candles. He found himself admiring her efficiency, but noticed that her fingers were trembling as she struck a match and her pale face was illuminated as the flame grew steady.

Wordlessly, he took the matches from her and lit several more candles while she melted wax and positioned them carefully in tarnished silver holders. The room grew lighter and the flames cast out strange shadows that flickered over the walls. He could see the results of what must have been a pretty intensive baking session, because on the table were plates of biscuits and a platter of those sweet things the English always ate at Christmastime. He frowned as he tried to remember what they were called. Mince pies, that was it.

'What do you think has happened?' she questioned.

He shrugged. 'A power line down? It can sometimes happen if there's a significant weight of snow.'

'But it can't!' She looked around, a touch of desperation in her voice. 'I've still got so much to do before my guests arrive.'

He sent her a wry look. 'Looks as though it's going to have to wait.'

A sudden silence fell and he noticed that her hand was trembling even more now.

'Hadn't you better go, before the snow gets much worse?' she said, in a casual tone that didn't quite come off. 'There must be someone waiting for you. Someone who's wondering where you are.'

Incredulously, he stared at her. 'And leave you here, on your own? Without electricity?' He walked over to one of the old-fashioned radiators and laid the flat of his hand on it. 'Or heating.'

'I'm perfectly capable of managing on my own,' she said stubbornly.

'I don't care,' he said. 'I'm not going anywhere. What kind of man would walk out and leave a woman to fend for herself in conditions like these?'

'So you're staying in order to ease your own conscience?'

There was a pause, and when he spoke his voice had a bitter note to it. 'Something like that.'

Livvy's heart thundered as she tried to work out what to do next. 'Don't panic' should have been top of her list, while the second should be to stop allowing Saladin to take control. Maybe where he came from, men dealt with emergencies while the women just hung around looking decorative. Well, perhaps it might do him good to realise that she didn't need a man to fix things for her. She didn't need a man for anything. She'd learned to change a fuse and fix a leaking tap. She'd managed alone for long enough and that was the way she liked it.

She walked over to the phone, which hung on a neat cradle on the wall, but was greeted with nothing but an empty silence as she placed it against her ear.

'Dead?' he questioned.

'Completely.' She replaced it and looked at him but, despite her best intentions, she *was* starting to panic. Had she, in the rush to buy the tree and hang the mistletoe and bake the mince pies, remembered to charge her cell phone? 'I'll go upstairs and get my phone.'

'I'll come with you.'

'Were you born to be bossy?'

'I think I was. Why, does it bother you?'

'Yes.'

'Tough,' he said as he picked up a candle.

But as they left the kitchen Saladin realised that for the first time in a long time he was feeling *exhilarated*. Nobody had a clue where he was. He was marooned in the middle of the snowy English countryside with a feisty redhead he suspected would be his before the night was over. And suddenly his conscience and his troubled memories were forgotten as he followed her up the large staircase leading from the arched reception hall, where the high ceilings flickered with long shadows cast from their candles. They reached her bedroom and Saladin drew in a deep breath as she pushed open the door and turned to him, a studiedly casual note in her voice.

'You can wait here, if you like.'

'Like a pupil standing outside the headmaster's study?' he drawled. 'No. I don't like. Don't worry, Livvy—I won't be judging you if your room's a mess and I think I'm sophisticated enough to resist the temptation to throw you down on the bed, if that's what you're worried about.'

'Oh, come in, if you insist,' she said crossly.

But it was with a feeling of pride that she opened the door and walked through, with Saladin not far behind her. The curtains were not yet drawn and the reflected light from the snow outside meant that the room looked almost radiant with a pure and ghostly light. On a table beside the bed stood a bowl of hyacinths, which scented the cold air. Antique pieces of furniture glowed softly in the candlelight. It was a place of peace and calm—her haven—and one of many reasons why she clung to this house and all the memories it contained.

She walked over to the window seat and found her phone, dejectedly staring down at its black screen.

'It's dead,' she said. 'I was sending photo messages to a school friend when the snow started and then they delivered the Christmas tree…' Her words tailed off. 'You'll have to go out to the car and get yours.'

'I will decide if and when I'm going out to the car,' he snapped. 'You do *not* issue instructions to a sheikh.'

'I didn't invite you here,' she said, her voice low. 'We're here together under duress and in extremely bizarre circumstances—and I think it's going to make an unbearable situation even worse if you then start pulling rank on me.'

He looked as if he was about to come back at her with a sharp response, but seemed to think better of it—because he nodded. 'Very well. I will go to the car and get my phone.'

He left the room abruptly, and as she heard him going downstairs she felt slightly spooked—a feeling that was only increased when the front door slammed. Everything seemed unnaturally quiet without him— all she could hear was the loud tick of the grandfather clock as it echoed through the house. She stared out of the window to see the sheikh's shadowy figure making its way towards a car that was now completely covered in white. The snow was still falling, and she found herself thinking that at least he'd had the sense to retrieve his cashmere coat and put it on before going outside.

She could see him brushing a thick layer of snow away from the door, which he was obviously having difficulty opening. She wondered what would happen next. Would crack teams of Jazratan guards descend in a helicopter from the snowy sky, the way they did in films? Doubtfully, she looked up at the fat flakes that were swirling down as thickly as ever. She didn't know much about planes, but she doubted it would be safe to fly in conditions like this.

Grabbing a sweater from the wardrobe and pulling it on, she went back downstairs to the kitchen and had just put a kettle on the hob when she heard the front door slam, followed by the sound of echoing footsteps. She looked up to see Saladin standing framed in the kitchen doorway and hated the instant rush of relief— and something else—that flooded through her. What was the something else? she wondered. The reassurance of having someone so unashamedly alpha strutting around the place, despite all her protestations that she was fine on her own? Or was the root cause more fundamental—a case of her body responding to him in away she wasn't used to? A way that *scared* her.

Despite the warm sweater she'd pulled on, she could feel the puckering of her breasts as she looked at him.

'Any luck?' she said.

'Some. I've spoken with my people—and the roads are impassable. We won't get any help sent out to us tonight.'

Livvy's hand trembled as she tipped boiling water into the teapot. They were stuck here for the night— just the two of them. So why wasn't she paralysed with a feeling of dread and fear? Why had her heart started pounding with excitement? She swallowed.

'Would you like some tea?'

'Please.' His voice grew curious. 'How have you managed to boil water?'

'Gas hob,' she said, thinking how *domesticated* this

all sounded. And how the words people spoke rarely reflected what was going on inside their heads. She looked into the gleam of his eyes. 'Are you hungry? I'll put some mince pies on a plate,' she said, in the kind of babbling voice people used when they were trying to fill an awkward silence. 'And we can go in and sit by the fire.'

'Here. Let me.' He took the tray from her, aware that this was something he rarely did. People always carried things for *him*. They ran his bath for him and laid out his cool silk robes every morning. For diplomatic meetings, all his paperwork was stacked in symmetrical piles awaiting his attention, even down to the gold pen that was always positioned neatly to the left. He didn't have to deal with the everyday mechanics of normal life, because his life was not normal. Never had been, nor ever could be. Even his response to tragedy could never be like other men's—for he'd been taught that the sheikh must never show emotion, no matter what he was feeling inside. So that when he had wanted to weep bitter tears over Alya's coffin, he had known that the face he'd needed to show to his people must be an implacable face.

His mouth hardened as he carried the tea tray to the room where the bare Christmas tree stood silhouetted against the window and watched as she sank down onto the silky rug. And suddenly the sweet wholesomeness of her made all his dark thoughts melt away.

The bulky sweater she was wearing emphasised her tiny frame and the slender legs that were tucked up neatly beneath her. The firelight had turned her titian ponytail into a stream of flaming red, and all he could think about was how much he wanted to see her naked...

So make it happen, he thought—as the pulse at his groin began to throb with anticipation. *Just make it happen*.

CHAPTER FOUR

'WE HAVE A long evening ahead of us, Livvy. Any idea of how you'd like to fill it?'

Livvy eyed Saladin warily as he drawled out his question, thinking that he was suddenly being almost *too* well behaved, and wondering why. She almost preferred him when he was being bossy and demanding, because that had infuriated her enough to create a natural barrier between them. A barrier behind which she felt safe.

But now?

Now he was being suspiciously compliant. He had drunk the tea she'd given him and eaten an accompanying mince pie—declaring it to be delicious and telling her he intended to take the recipe back for the palace chefs, so that his courtiers and guests could enjoy the English delicacy. He had even dragged a whole pile of logs back from the woodshed and heaped them into the big basket beside the fire.

Despite the thickness of her sweater, a shiver ran down her spine as she watched him. His body was hard and muscular and he moved with the grace of a natural athlete. He handled the logs as if they were no heavier than twigs and somehow made the task look effortless. Livvy was proud of her independence and her insistence on doing the kind of jobs that some of her married school friends turned up their noses at. She never baulked at taking out the rubbish or sweeping the gravel drive. She happily carried logs and weeded the garden whenever she had time, but she couldn't deny that it felt like an unexpected luxury to be waited on like this. To lean back against the cushioned footstool sipping her tea, watching Saladin Al Mektala sort out the fire for her. He made her feel...*pampered*, and he made her feel feminine.

She considered his question.

'We could always play a game,' she suggested.

'Good idea.' His dark eyes assumed the natural glint of the predator. 'I love playing games.'

Nobody had ever accused Livvy of sophistication, but neither was she stupid. She'd worked for a long time in the testosterone-filled industry of horse racing and had been engaged to a very tricky man. She'd learned the hard way how womanising men flirted and used innuendo. And the only way to keep it in check was to ignore it. So she ignored the flare of light that had made the sheikh's eyes gleam like glowing coal and subjected him to a look of cool question. 'Scrabble?' she asked. 'Or cards?'

'Whichever you choose,' he said. 'Although I must warn you now that I shall beat you.'

'Is that supposed to be a challenge I can't resist?'

'Let's see, shall we?'

To Livvy's fury, his arrogant prediction proved correct. He won every game they played and even beat her at Scrabble—something at which she normally excelled.

Trying not to be a bad sport, she dropped the pen onto the score sheet. 'So how come you've managed to beat me at a word game that isn't even in your native tongue?' she said.

'Because when I was a little boy I had an English tutor who taught me that a rich vocabulary was something within the grasp of all men. And I was taught to win. It's what Al Mektala men do. We never like to fail. At anything.'

'So you're always triumphant?'

He turned his head to look at her and Livvy's heart missed a beat as she saw something flickering within the dark blaze of his eyes that didn't look like arrogance. Was she imagining the trace of sorrow she saw there—or the lines around his mouth, which suddenly seemed to have deepened?

'No,' he said harshly. 'A long time ago I failed at something quite spectacularly.'

'At what?'

'Something better left in the past, where it belongs.' His voice grew cold and distant as he threw another log onto the fire, and when he turned back Livvy saw that his features had become shuttered. 'Tell me something about you instead,' he said.

She shrugged. 'There's not very much to tell. I'm twenty-nine and I run a bed and breakfast business from the house in which I was born. My love life you already seem well acquainted with. Anything else you want to know?'

'Yes.' His hawklike features were gilded by the flicker of the firelight as he leaned forward. 'Why did he jilt you?'

She met the searching blaze of his black eyes. 'You really think I'd tell *you*?'

He raised his dark brows. 'Why not? I'm curious. And after the snow clears, you'll never see me again— that is, if you really are determined to turn down my offer of a job. Isn't that what people do in circumstances such as these? They tell each other secrets.'

As she considered his words, Livvy wondered how he saw her. As some sad spinster who'd tucked herself away in the middle of nowhere, far away from the fast-paced world she'd once inhabited? And if that was the case, then wasn't this an ideal opportunity to show him that she *liked* the life she'd chosen—to show him she was completely over Rupert?

But if you're over him—then how come you still shut out men? How come you must be the only twenty-nine-year-old virgin on the planet?

The uncomfortable trajectory of her thoughts made her bold. *So let it go*, she told herself. *Let the past go by setting it free.* 'Do you know Rupert de Vries?' she asked slowly.

'I met him a couple of times—back in the day, as they say.' His mouth twisted. 'I didn't like him.'

'You don't have to say that just to make me feel better.'

'I can assure you that I never say things I don't mean, Livvy.' There was a pause. 'What happened?'

She stared down at the rug, trying to concentrate on the symmetrical shapes that were woven into the silk. She pictured Rupert's face—something she hadn't done for a long time—fine boned and fair and the antithesis of the tawny sheikh in front of her. She remembered how she couldn't believe that the powerful racing figure had taken an interest in *her*, the lowliest of grooms at the time. 'I expect you know that he ran a very successful yard for a time.'

'Until he got greedy,' Saladin said, stretching his legs out in front of him. 'He overextended himself and that was a big mistake. You should always keep something back when you're dealing with horses, no matter how brilliant they are. Because ultimately they are flesh and blood—and flesh and blood is always vulnerable.'

She heard the sudden rawness in his voice and wondered if he was thinking about Burkaan. 'Yes,' she said.

'So how come it got as far as you standing at the altar before he got cold feet?' Black eyes bored into her. 'That's what happened, isn't it? Didn't he talk to you about it beforehand—let you know he was having doubts?'

Livvy shook her head as her mind raced back to that chaotic period. At the time she'd done that thing of trying to salvage her pride by telling everyone with a brisk cheerfulness that it was much better to find out *before* the wedding, rather than after it. That it would have been unbearable if Rupert had decided he wanted out a few years and a few children down the line. But those had been things she'd felt *obliged* to say, so that she wouldn't come over as bitter. The truth was that the rejection had left her feeling hollow…and stupid. Not only had she been completely blind to her fiancé's transgressions, but there had been all the practical considerations, too. Like paying the catering staff who were standing around in their aprons in the deserted marquee almost bursting with excitement at the *drama* of it all. And informing the driver of the limousine firm that they wouldn't be needing a lift to the airport after all. And cancelling the honeymoon, which she'd paid for and for which Rupert had been supposed to settle up with her afterwards. He never had, of course, and the wedding that never was had ended up costing her a lot more than injured pride.

And once the initial humiliation was over and everyone had been paid off, she had made a vow never to talk about it. She'd told herself that if she fed the story it would grow. So she'd cut off people's questions and deliberately changed the subject and dared them to continue to pursue it, and eventually people had got the message.

But now she looked into the gleam of Saladin's eyes and realised that there had been a price to pay for her silence. She suddenly recognised how deeply she had buried the truth and saw that if she continued to keep it hidden away, she risked making herself an eternal victim. The truth was that she was over Rupert and glad she hadn't married him. So why act like someone with a dirty secret—why not get it out into the open and watch it wither and die as it was exposed to the air?

'Because I allowed myself to do what women are so good at doing,' she said slowly. 'I allowed myself to be wooed by a very persuasive man, without stopping to consider why someone like him should be interested in someone like me.'

His eyes narrowed. 'What's that supposed to mean?'

'Oh, come on, Saladin—you haven't held back from being blunt, so why start now? He was known for dating glamorous women and I'm not. The only thing I had to commend me was the fact that my father owned a beautiful house. This house. My mother was dead and my stepmother long gone—and since I don't have any brothers or sisters, I stood to inherit everything. From where Rupert was sitting, it must have looked a very attractive proposition and I think he made the assumption that there was lots of money sitting in a bank account somewhere—the kind of money that could have bailed out his failing business.'

'But there wasn't?'

'At some point there was. Before my stepmother got her hands on it and decided to blow a lot of it on diamonds and plastic surgery and then demand a massive divorce settlement. By the time my father died there was nothing left—not after I'd paid for the nurses who helped care for him in his final years.'

'You didn't think to tell de Vries that?'

Livvy gave a snarl of a laugh as she picked up the poker and gave the fire a vicious stab. 'Most brides labour under the illusion that they're being married for love, not money. It would look a bit pathetic, don't you think, if one were to have a conversation on the lines of, "Look, I've just discovered that I'm broke—but you do still love me, don't you?" And the truth of it was that I didn't realise how little money there was—at least, not until just before the wedding.'

'And then you told him?'

'I told him,' she agreed. She would never forget the look on her prospective groom's face. That leaching of colour that had left him with a curiously waxy complexion and the fleeting look of horror in his eyes. In that illuminating moment Livvy hadn't been able to decide who she was angrier with—Rupert, for his unbelievable shallowness, or herself for having been too blind to see it before. Maybe she just hadn't wanted to see.

'I told him and he didn't like it. I wish he'd told me right then that he'd changed his mind, so that I wouldn't have to go through the whole pantomime of dressing up in a big white frock with my bridesmaids flapping around me in nervous excitement. But obviously that was something he couldn't face doing. So there.' She looked at him defiantly. 'Have you got the whole picture now?'

There was silence for a moment—the firelight flickering over his ebony hair as he studied her. 'Not quite,' he said.

Defensively, she stiffened. 'You want a blow-by-blow account of my subsequent meltdown?'

He shook his head. 'I meant that not everything you said is true.'

His words were softer than before, as if they'd suddenly been brushed with velvet. Or silk. Yet despite their softness, all the time Livvy was aware of the underlying steel underpinning them, and that made him sound even more attractive. Dangerously so.

'Which bit in particular?'

He smiled. 'That you have nothing to commend you other than a house.'

'Oh, really?'

Saladin heard the disbelief in her voice and felt a surge of rage that someone as worthless as de Vries had smashed her confidence and made her hide herself away like this.

'Yes, really.' His gaze drifted over her. 'Would you like me to list your more obvious attributes?'

Splaying her hands over her hips, she struck a pose. 'My old jeans and sweater?'

'Your complexion, for a start, which makes me think

of honey and cream.' His voice dipped. 'And, of course, your freckles.'

Her fingers strayed to her nose. 'I hate my freckles.'

'Of course you do, but in my country they are highly prized. We call them kisses from the sun.'

'Well, that's certainly not what we call them here.' She gave a nervous laugh and then shivered, as if she had only just registered the sudden plummet in temperature. 'It's cold,' she said, rubbing her hands up and down her arms. 'I should go and make us something to eat.'

'I'm not hungry.'

'You must be. I am. Starving, in fact.'

He could hear the lie in her voice as she jumped to her feet and picked up one of the candles, as if she couldn't wait to escape from the sudden intimacy that had sprung up between them.

'I'll come and help you,' he said.

'No.' The word was sharp, before she pulled it back with a smile. 'I'd prefer to do it on my own. Really. You stay here. You look very comfortable.'

He knew why she was trying to put distance between them and that it was a futile exercise. Didn't she realise that her darkened eyes gave her away and her body was betraying all the signs of sexual excitement? He felt the hard beat of anticipation cradling his groin and suddenly the bright beat of sexual excitement burned out everything except the anticipation of pleasure. 'Don't be long,' he said softly.

Livvy felt almost *helpless* as she made her way towards the kitchen through the now distinctly chilly corridors. She couldn't believe she'd just blurted out all that stuff—to Saladin, of all people—and wondered how he'd managed to cut through her defences so effectively. But he had. She had been surprised at his understanding—and then suspicious of it, because it made her feel vulnerable. And she didn't want to feel vulnerable. She didn't want to feel any of the stuff that was raging through her body like wildfire. As if she would die if he didn't touch her. As if her life wouldn't be complete unless she knew what it was like to have Saladin Al Mektala take her in his arms and kiss her.

Because she had made that mistake once before. She'd fallen for a powerful man who was way out of her league—and it was not something she intended repeating.

She set about preparing food she suspected neither of them wanted, putting a plate of newly baked bread onto a tray along with some cheese from the local shop, and adding some rosy apples that she absently polished with a cloth. She wondered if he drank wine but decided against it, making coffee instead. Wine was the last thing either of them needed.

When she returned to the drawing room, he hadn't moved from where he'd been sitting. In fact, his eyes were closed and he was so still that she thought he might have fallen asleep. For a moment she just stood there looking at him, trying to take in the unbelievable scene that lay before her. A real-life king was stretched out in front of *her* fire, his ebony head resting against the faded crimson silk of the brocade chair. He looked powerful and exotic—dominating his surroundings with a brooding sensuality, which shimmered from his powerful frame. His long legs were sprawled out in front of him and the material of his trousers was flattened down over the hard bulge of his thighs. And

all her best intentions melted away because just looking at him made her want him—and it was *wrong* to
want him.

Suddenly he opened his eyes and the crockery on
the tray she was holding began to jangle as her hands
began to tremble. Livvy hoped he hadn't noticed the
rush of blood that was making her cheeks burn, but
she was aware of the glint of amusement in his eyes
as she walked across the room towards the fire. She
waited for him to make some smart comment, but he
said nothing—just watched in silence as she put the
tray down. Her heart was pounding as she sat down
on the rug beside him and tried to behave casually.

'Help yourself,' she said.

'Help yourself?' There was a pause. 'But I am used
to someone serving me, Livvy.'

She heard the mockery in his voice and she turned
her head to catch the provocative gleam in his eyes.
He's flirting with me, she thought. And no way was she
going to flirt back. 'I'm sure you are,' she said crisply.
'But something tells me you are a man who is perfectly
capable of looking after himself.'

Saladin smiled, wondering if she was aware that
her attitude was slowly sealing her fate. If she had
been submissive and eager to please—as women always were—then his desire might now have faded. But
she wasn't being in the least bit submissive. She was
sitting munching her way through an apple, though
she didn't look as if she was particularly enjoying it—
and her body had stiffened with a defiance that he
couldn't resist.

He could feel the sudden beat of anticipation. Apart
from the protected virgins in his homeland who were

expected to remain pure until marriage, he couldn't think of a single woman in this situation who wouldn't be coming on to him by now. She was a challenge—in a world where few challenges remained. Shifting his position slightly, he tried to alleviate some of the pressure on his rapidly hardening groin.

She had thrown the apple core into the fire and was holding out her hands in front of the flames again, spreading her fingers wide. They were *working* hands, he thought, and something made him lean over and pour coffee for them both—though she took hers with a look of surprise she couldn't quite disguise.

He watched as she ate a little bread and cheese, but he took no food himself and eventually she pushed her plate away.

'You're not eating,' she said.

'I told you I wasn't hungry.'

She hugged her arms around her knees and looked at him. 'So now what do we do? More Scrabble? Or do you want to try calling up your people to see if the roads are clear?'

'Forget about my people,' he said impatiently, his gaze straying to the pinpoint tips of her nipples. 'You're cold.'

Livvy saw the direction of his glance—bold, appraising and unashamed—and felt the instant quickening of her body in response. Her heart was fluttering as if it was trying to escape from the confinement of her ribcage, and she knew exactly what she should do. She should say goodnight and go upstairs to her icy bedroom and stay there until the morning brought snow ploughs, or his private helicopter or *something* to rescue them from their incarceration.

But she didn't. She stayed exactly where she was, seated on the rug, gazing back at him—as if she had no idea what was going to happen next. Yet despite her lack of experience and the sheer impossibility of the situation, she knew exactly what was about to happen because it was happening right now. Saladin Al Mektala was putting his hand on her shoulder and pulling her close before bending his head to kiss her.

Livvy reeled at that first sweet taste as he began to explore her mouth with the flickering tip of his tongue, and a great wave of desire and emotion swept through her in a stupefying rush. As his arms tightened around her she felt safe. She could taste coffee on his tongue and feel the warmth of his breath as he anchored her head to deepen the kiss and she opened her mouth beneath his seeking lips. His fingertips moved to whisper their way over her neck, but the first touch of his hand to her breast made her freeze as she wondered just what he would expect from her.

She knew exactly what he would expect from her— and it was a million miles away from the reality of what he would actually get. And wouldn't he be horrified if he knew the truth?

'Saladin—' The word came out as a barely intelligible sound as she broke the kiss.

'You're now going to list all the reasons why we shouldn't do this?' he said unsteadily.

'Yes.'

'Starting with what? Lack of desire?' He grazed the pad of his thumb over her bottom lip and it trembled wildly in response. 'I don't think so.'

With an effort she jerked away from him, her words tumbling out of her mouth as she struggled to do the right thing. 'Starting with the fact that you're a sheikh and I'm a commoner and we don't really know each other.'

'Something that can be solved in an instant,' he said unevenly.

'In fact, we don't even seem to *like* one another,' she continued. 'We've done nothing but argue since you arrived.'

'But conflict can make sex so piquant, don't you think?' he murmured. 'Such a blessed relief when all that tension is finally broken.'

Livvy didn't answer. She didn't dare. Would he laugh if he realised the truth? And now he was reaching behind her head to tug the elastic band from her ponytail—and she was letting him. Sitting there perfectly still as her hair spilled down over her shoulders and his eyes narrowed with appreciation.

'You could probably come up with a whole stack of reasons why we shouldn't,' he said. 'But there's one thing that cancels out every one of your objections.'

She knew she shouldn't, but Livvy asked it all the same. 'Which is?'

'Because we want to. Very, very badly. At least, I do. How about you?'

Livvy shut her eyes, afraid that she would be swayed by the desire that burned so blackly from his eyes. *Because we want to.* How simple that sounded to someone who hadn't followed her own desires for so long that she'd forgotten how. But maybe that was because she hadn't ever been tempted before—at least, not like this. After she had behaved so circumspectly with Rupert, his betrayal had come as a complete shock and had made her question her own judgement. She'd been cautious of men—and wary. After she'd packed up her wedding dress and sent it off to raise money for charity, she had felt empty inside—as if there were a space there that could never be filled. She had begun to think there was something wrong with her. That she wasn't like other women.

But now...

Now there was a hot storm of need within her and she felt anything was possible. That the powerful sheikh had all the knowledge required to give her pleasure. And was it such a terrible thing to want pleasure when it had been denied to her for so long?

She tipped her head back to expose her neck to him and instantly he covered it with a path of tiny kisses. Beneath the sweater, she could feel the increasing weight of her breasts and the denim of her jeans scraping against her newly sensitive thighs as sexual hunger began to pulse through her.

'Saladin,' she said again, her voice a throaty invitation as she felt his hand move slowly down her ribcage towards her waist.

'You are very overdressed, *habibi*,' he observed, peeling the sweater over her head with effortless dexterity.

Livvy held her breath with trepidation as he began to unbutton the shirt underneath and she wondered if he would be turned off by her boring white bra, because a man like this would surely be used to fine underwear. But he didn't appear to notice any obvious deficiencies in the lingerie department as he peeled away her shirt—he seemed too intent on bending his dark head to her exposed skin and she shivered again as she felt his tongue slide over her breastbone, leaving a moist trail behind.

'Your body is so tiny,' he said as he edged his fingers beneath the waistband of her jeans. 'I don't think I've ever been with a woman who is so small.'

And that was when reality hit her like an invisible punch to the solar plexus. She was making out with a man she barely knew. A ruthless sheikh who exuded a dark and dangerous sensuality—and she was seconds away from succumbing to him. Heart pounding, she wrenched herself away, grabbing at her scattered clothes and scrambling to her feet as he stared up at her with dazed disbelief.

'What's going on?' he demanded.

She began to button up her shirt with shaking fingers. 'Isn't it obvious? I'm stopping this before it goes any further.'

He raked his fingers through his hair, his expression one of impatience and frustration. 'I thought we'd already had this conversation,' he growled.

'It's an ongoing conversation,' she said, sucking in an unsteady breath. 'On every level, this would be a mistake and it's not going to happen. We're two people from completely different worlds, who won't ever see one another again once the snow melts. It seems you're stuck here until help arrives, but there's nothing we can do about it. We'll just have to make the best of a bad situation. Just so you know—there are seven bedrooms in this house and you're welcome to sleep in any of them.' She glared at him. 'Just stay out of mine.'

CHAPTER FIVE

SALADIN WAS CUPPING her breast again, only this time it was completely bare. His palm was massaging the peaking nipple and Livvy made a mewing little sound of pleasure.

'Please,' she moaned softly. 'Oh, Saladin. Please.'

He didn't answer, but now his hand was circling her belly—slowly and rhythmically—before drifting down towards the soft tangle of curls at her thighs and coming to a tantalising halt. Her throat dried as the molten heat continued to build and she felt her thighs part in silent invitation. *Just do it*, she prayed silently. *Forget all those stupid objections I put in your way. I was stupid and uptight and life is too short. I don't care whether it's right or wrong, I just want you.*

She opened her mouth to call his name again when she heard the loud bang of a door somewhere in the distance and she woke with a start, blinking in horror as she looked around, her heart banging against her ribcage like a frenzied drum. Disorientated and bewildered, she tried to work out what had happened, before the truth hit her. She was in her bedroom at Wightwick Manor with her hand between her legs, about to call

out Saladin's name—and she'd never felt so sexually
excited in her life.

Whipping the duvet away, she was relieved to see
that the other side of the bed was smooth and unslept
in—although her pyjama bottoms were uncharacter-
istically bunched up into a small bundle at the bottom
of the bed. Heart still racing, she grabbed them and
slithered them on, still trying to make sense of the
warm lethargy and pervading sense of arousal that
was threatening to overwhelm her. *So don't let it*, she
told herself fiercely. *Just calm down and try to work
out what's going on.*

Jumping out of bed, she scooted over to the windows
and pulled back the heavy curtains—her heart per-
forming a complicated kind of somersault as she looked
outside. Because there, on the snow-laden lawns, was
her sweetest dream and worst nightmare all rolled into
one. Saladin Al Mektala knee-deep in snow. The man
she'd dreamed about so vividly that she'd woken up
believing he was in bed with her was outside, shovelling snow like a labourer.

He'd managed to find a spade from somewhere and
had cleared the path leading to the front door, although
the rest of the landscape was still banked with white.
More snow must have fallen overnight and the beautiful gardens were unrecognisable—blotted out by a
mantle that was so bright it hurt the eyes. Livvy blinked
against the cold whiteness of the light. And once again,
that sense of unreality washed over her, because it was
beyond *weird* to see the desert-dwelling king standing in the middle of the snowy English countryside.

He must have found himself a pair of the welling-
tons she always kept for the guests in case they wanted

to go walking—because, in her experience, nobody ever brought the correct footwear with them. She wondered why he hadn't put on one of the waterproof jackets, because surely it was insane to be shovelling snow in a cashmere coat that must have cost as much as her monthly heating bill.

She was about to duck away from the window when he looked up, as if her presence had alerted him to the fact he was being watched. He was too far away for her to be able to read his expression correctly—and Livvy told herself she was imagining the glint of mischief in his eyes. Was she? With a small howl of rage, she turned away and headed for the freezing bathroom just along the corridor—only to discover that the lights still weren't working.

After a brief and icy shower, her worried thoughts ran round and round, like a hamster on a wheel. It *had* just been a dream, hadn't it? The aching breasts and heavy pelvis and the hazy memories of him in bed with her were all just the legacy of an overworked imagination, weren't they? Probably her subconscious reacting to the way he'd kissed her by the fire.

Pulling on a black sweater over her jeans, she piled up her hair into a topknot, wondering why he'd made a pass at her in the first place. Maybe she looked like someone who was crying out for a little affection. Or maybe he'd just felt sorry for her when she'd told him about Rupert.

He was arrogant and infuriating and dangerous and yet, when she closed her eyes, all she could remember was the sweet seduction of his kiss as he'd pulled her against his hard body.

She ran downstairs and checked the phone but the lines were still down. Which meant...

Meant...

The front door slammed and Saladin walked in, looking as if the wintry wilds of the snowy English countryside were his natural habitat. His golden skin was glowing after the physical exertion of shovelling snow, and Livvy flushed a deep pink as embarrassment coursed through her. Because suddenly all she could think about was her dream and how vivid it had felt. And it *was* a dream, wasn't it?

'Where did you sleep?' she questioned—and wasn't part of her terrified he'd answer 'in your bed'? That he would sardonically inform her that the reason the dreams had been so vivid was because they were real...

'Aren't you supposed to enquire *how* I slept, rather than where?' he questioned coolly, removing a pair of leather gloves and dropping them on a table. 'Isn't that the usual role of the hostess?'

She forced a smile. 'Okay. Let's start again. How did you sleep?'

'For a time I slept the sleep of the just,' he drawled, raking his fingers back through black hair that was damp with melting snow. 'But that was before you woke me up.'

Livvy's throat dried as she stared at him in growing horror. 'I *woke you up*?'

'Indeed you did.' He flicked her a glance from between the dark forest of his lashes. 'You were shouting something in your sleep.'

Her rosy flush was now a distant memory. She could feel all the colour leaching from her face and knew from past experience that her freckles would be standing out as if someone had spattered mud all over her skin. 'What,' she croaked, 'was I shouting?'

There was a split-second pause. 'At first I thought it was my name until I decided I was probably mistaken—given the abrupt way you drew the evening to a conclusion,' he said, his eyes sending out some sort of coded message she couldn't decipher. 'But I thought I'd better get up and investigate anyway.'

Livvy's heart pounded. 'Right,' she said breathlessly.

'So I walked along the corridor to your room, and you shouted it again but this time there could be no mistake, because it was very definitely my name and you were saying it as if you were in some kind of pain. Or something.' His eyes glittered. 'So I turned the door handle and...'

'And?' she squeaked, hating the way he had deliberately paused for dramatic effect.

He glimmered her a smile. 'And I discovered that you'd locked yourself in.'

'So I had,' she remembered, breathing out a shaky sigh of relief.

'Of course—' his eyes narrowed but she couldn't mistake the dangerous glint sparking from their ebony depths '—if there had been any real danger, no door would have kept me out—locked or otherwise. In the circumstances, I can't quite decide whether you were being prudent or paranoid. What did you think was going to happen, Livvy—that I was going to force my way into your room in the middle of the night, all on the strength of one little kiss?'

'Of course not,' she said stiffly, wondering if her words sounded as unconvincing to him as they did to her. What if she *had* left her door unlocked and he'd come running when she'd called out his name? It wasn't beyond the realms of possibility that she would have reached out for him, was it? Grabbed at him and kissed him as hungrily as before. It wouldn't take much of a leap of the imagination to work out what would have happened next...

She wanted to bury her face in her hands, or close her eyes and find that when she opened them he would be gone—taking with him all these confusing thoughts and this gnawing sense of frustration. But that wasn't going to happen, and it was vital she acted as if it was no big deal. As if it had been just *one little kiss*—as he had said so dismissively.

'I certainly didn't mean to disrupt your night,' she said.

'I can live with it,' he said softly. 'Would you like some coffee? There's a pot brewing in the kitchen.'

'You've made coffee?' she questioned.

'Last night you told me to make myself at home. You also made it very clear that you weren't going to wait on me, so it seems I shall have to fend for myself.'

He turned on his heel and began walking towards the kitchen, and Livvy felt obliged to follow him, wondering indignantly how he had managed to assume such a powerful sense of ownership in *her* home.

By daylight and without the mysterious glow of candles, the kitchen seemed a far less threatening environment than it had done last night. Livvy sat down at the table and watched as he poured coffee with the same dexterity as he'd demonstrated when removing her sweater. Oh, God—he'd taken off her sweater. And her shirt. Briefly, she shut her eyes. He would have taken off even more if she hadn't stopped him.

So stop letting him take control. Tell him he's got to stop shovelling snow and making coffee and to concentrate on getting himself out of here as soon as possible. She needed to remember that the response he evoked in her was purely visceral, and it would soon pass. He'd kissed her and made her feel good, and so her body wanted him to do it all over again. It was as simple as that—and it was to be avoided at all costs.

'So did you get through to your people?' she questioned.

Saladin slid the cup towards her. 'I did. On a very bad line and with a low battery, but yes. Sugar?'

'Just milk, thanks.' She took the coffee. 'And they're coming to get you, I presume?'

'Unfortunately, it's not quite that easy,' he said smoothly. 'Several trees are down and some of the lanes are blocked, and all the gritting lorries are needed for the arterial roads.'

Livvy only just avoided choking on her second mouthful of coffee. 'What does that mean?'

Saladin shrugged. He wondered if she realised he could have commandeered a whole fleet of gritting lorries with a click of his fingers—plus a helicopter prepared to swoop down and fly him away to anywhere he chose to go.

But he wasn't planning on leaving. At least, not yet. Not until she'd agreed to accompany him to Jazratan. And he realised there was something else that was making him stay put—and that was a desire for her so intense that he couldn't look at her without his groin aching. 'It means I'm staying here, Livvy,' he said.

Her eyes widened with alarm and with something else—something that was easily recognisable as desire. He could see it in the self-conscious way her body stiffened whenever he approached. He had tasted it in that amazing firelight kiss last night even if—incredibly—she had turned him down afterwards. And it pleased him that her hunger matched his, even if her reluctance to have sex with him astonished him. Did she realise that resisting him was only fuelling his determination to join with her? Why, he could have exploded with frustration and excitement when she'd banished him to his bedroom and barricaded herself into her own room last night. For passion-fuelled seconds he'd actually considered behaving as one of his ancestors would have done and broken down the door—before sanity had prevailed and he had slunk away with a sense of disbelief and a throbbing groin.

'You're staying here?' she echoed as a series of conflicting emotions crossed over her freckled face.

'It would seem so.'

'For how long?'

'Until it's safe to leave.'

'Surely someone like you could call for a helicopter,' she objected. 'I can't believe that the sheikh of Jazratan, with all his power and influence, is stuck in the snow in the English countryside.'

He smiled, because this was something else he wasn't used to. People usually did everything to entice him to stay because they loved the cachet of having a royal in their presence. They didn't stare at him with a mulish expression on their face, not bothering to hide their wish to see him gone. 'Anything is *possible*,' he mused. 'But you wouldn't want me to put one of my pilots at risk, would you, Livvy—just because having me around makes you feel uncomfortable?'

She licked her lips, as if his soft tone had temporarily disarmed her—which was precisely what he intended it to do.

'You don't make me feel uncomfortable.'

Their eyes met.

'Well, then,' he said softly. 'There isn't a problem, is there?'

She glared at him and Saladin felt a heady sense of triumph. Surely she must realise by now that that resistance was futile?

'Just so you know,' she said, glancing up at the wall clock, 'I have things to do and I can't stand around entertaining you all day.'

'If this is what you term as entertainment, I'm happy to pass.'

She slanted him a furious look. 'I have to work on the assumption that the weather is going to clear and that my guests will be arriving on schedule.'

'So let me help you.'

Livvy put down her cup with a clatter. *'How?'*

'Are there logs that need chopping?'

'You chop logs?'

'Yes, I chop logs, Livvy. Or do you think I lie around on silken cushions all day doing nothing?'

'I have no idea. I hadn't given your daily routine a moment's thought.'

Exaggeratedly, he ran his hand slowly down over his biceps. 'You don't get a body like this by just lying around all day.'

'That's the most outrageous boast I've ever heard!'

He smiled. 'So? Logs?'

'A man from the village chops them.' She got up from the table. 'But you can bring some through to the drawing room from the big pile in the storehouse if you like. That would be very helpful. And if you'd like to light the fire, that would also be helpful.'

'And then?'

'Then I'm decorating the Christmas tree.'

She flung the words out like a challenge.

'Ah,' he said. 'Something at which I am a complete novice, which means you can order me round to your heart's content. I'm sure that will give you immense pleasure, won't it, Livvy? You seem to enjoy taking control.'

He watched as she appeared to bite back what she was about to say. She looked as if she wanted to tell him to go to hell.

'I suppose you can hold the ladder for me,' she said, and he almost laughed as she bit out the ungracious response.

Half an hour later he found himself gripping the sides of a ladder while she hauled dusty boxes from the loft and handed them to him. Saladin stared down at different labelled boxes bearing the words *Baubles* and *Tinsel* with the sense of a man entering uncharted territory. He had never decorated a Christmas tree in his life—it wasn't a holiday they celebrated in Jazratan—and unexpectedly he found he was enjoying himself.

From his position at the foot of the stepladder, he was able to study the slender curves of Livvy's body, and from this angle her jeans certainly looked a lot more flattering. Every step up the ladder hugged the denim against the curve of her buttocks and outlined each slender thigh. His gaze travelled up to the back of her neck, which was pale and dusted with a few freckles. He wondered if she had deliberately put her hair into that topknot, knowing he would want to remove the single clip that held it in place. So that it would tumble around her shoulders like a fall of flame, the way it had done last night...

Last night.

He swallowed as she leaned out to attach a sparkly silver ball to the end of a branch, his hands again gripping the sides of the ladder—not quite sure which of them he was keeping steady. He'd lied to her about sleeping well because the truth was that he'd barely slept at all—especially when he'd realised she'd meant what she said, and that she wouldn't be sharing a bed with him. In the silence of his icy room, he'd kept reliving their fireside kiss—thinking how unexpectedly *erotic* it had been. His fierce hunger for her had taken him by surprise—because nobody could deny that she was a very unassuming creature—but just as surprising was her determination to resist him.

At first he'd thought she was joking. Or that she was playing the old, familiar game because women often believed that a man was more likely to commit if they played hard to get. He gave a cynical smile. But if that was her plan then she was wasting her time, because there would be no commitment from him other than the guarantee of pleasure. His mouth hardened and his heart clenched with pain. He had walked that path before and he would not be setting foot on it again.

'Could you hand me that angel, please?'

Angel? Livvy's voice broke into his uncomfortable thoughts and Saladin picked up the figure she was pointing to—a plastic doll wearing a crudely sewn dress. A tiny ring of tinsel wreathed the flaxen hair, and she was holding a foil-covered matchstick, which he assumed was meant to be a wand.

'Homemade?' he ventured wryly, as he held it out towards her.

She hesitated before giving a brief, sad smile. 'I made it with my mum.'

That smile touched something deep inside him and he found himself wanting to kiss her again, but her rapid ascent up the ladder was clearly intended to terminate the conversation, and maybe that was best. *Yes, definitely for the best*, he told himself. Instead, he forced himself to concentrate on the way she brought the bare tree to life by heaping on the glittering baubles and tinsel while the fire crackled and spat. It was one of the most innocent ways he'd ever spent a morning, and Saladin was overcome by an unexpected wave of emotion, because wasn't it captivating to find a woman whose main focus wasn't sex? How long since he'd been in the company of a female who was behaving with restraint and with decorum? Not since Alya, he thought—and a wave of guilt washed over him as he made the comparison.

'Be careful,' he growled as she began to back her way down the ladder.

'I am being careful.'

But suddenly, he was not. He was giving in to what he could no longer resist. He caught hold of her as she made that last step and his hand closed over hers, and to his surprise she didn't pull away from him. She just stared at him as he turned her hand over and raised it slowly to his lips, his tongue snaking out over her palm to slowly lick at the salty flesh.

'Saladin,' she whispered, but he could see that her eyes had darkened.

'Don't talk anymore, because I'm going to kiss you,' he said, his voice deepening with sudden urgency. 'But you already know that, don't you, Livvy? You know that's what I have been longing to do since I got up this morning.'

As a stalling device it was pathetic, but Livvy said it all the same, lifting her gaze to the bare ceiling. 'There's supposed to be mistletoe,' she whispered.

'Damn the mistletoe,' he ground out as his head came down towards hers.

CHAPTER SIX

ONE KISS, LIVVY told herself as Saladin's mouth claimed hers. One kiss and no more. Just like last night—it didn't have to lead anywhere. She could call a halt to it any time she liked.

But deep down she knew she was fooling herself—because this felt *different*. Last night had been all about candlelight and firelight and a sense of other-worldliness that had descended on them as they'd sat around the sparking logs. Restaurants didn't dim the lights for no reason and call it *mood lighting*, did they?

But today...

In the cold clear light of today, in the harsh and blinding reflection of newly fallen snow—there was nothing but rawness and reality. And hunger. Oh, yes. A fierce hunger that had been building all night—even while she slept—and that was being fed by the sweet seduction of Saladin's kiss as he began to explore her mouth. He kissed her softly at first, and then he kissed hard and long and deep—with a warm urgency that was contagious. And she wanted him. She wanted him more than she'd ever wanted anything, because this was like nothing she'd ever experienced before.

Wrapping her fingers around his neck, she kissed

him back and, although he held her very tightly, it was almost as if she were floating free. She felt soft. Boneless. As if every point of her body was a pleasure point. As if every inch of her skin was an erogenous zone. Wherever Saladin touched her she felt on fire. With each kiss he dragged her deeper into the silken web he was weaving. At some point she thought she must have groaned because suddenly he pulled back, sucking in a ragged breath, his eyes as bright as a man with a fever.

'Here?' he questioned succinctly. 'Or upstairs?'

It was a brutal question that killed off some of the romance she'd been feeling, but at least it was *real* and at least there could be no misinterpretation about his intentions. He wasn't dressing it up to be something it wasn't. This was sex, pure and simple. He wasn't *lying* to her, was he?

'Can't decide?' he murmured, and, when she didn't answer, he began to nuzzle her neck.

She tipped her head back while she skated through the possibilities. The bed would be better. She could hide beneath the concealing weight of the duvet, couldn't she? But this wasn't supposed to be about *hiding*. This was about taking control of her own destiny. About taking something she really wanted for once, instead of being influenced by other people's expectations.

She realised he was waiting for an answer, and her heart missed a beat as she stared into the blackness of his eyes. He was the wrong man on so many levels, but did that matter? Doing the *right* thing had never worked out for her, had it? Maybe it was time to run full tilt at glorious fantasy and forget all about reality for once, because this gorgeous man wanted to make love to *her*.

And when some bone-deep instinct warned her that he was capable of inflicting pain—real emotional pain, far worse, she suspected, than any she'd suffered with Rupert—she reminded herself that she was a different person now. She was no longer that innocent bride who looked at the world through rose-tinted glasses. She was independent and she could handle this. So what the hell was she waiting for?

'Here,' she managed from between swollen lips. 'I want to do it here.'

He brought his head down as if to seal her intention with another kiss, but she sensed his growing impatience as he led her over to the fire and pulled her close—close enough for her to feel every sinew of his powerful body. Pulling the pin from her hair, he watched as it tumbled around her shoulders.

'Your hair is like fire,' he murmured, letting silky strands slide through his fingers. 'You should wear it down all the time.'

She opened her mouth to tell him it wouldn't be practical but her words were forgotten as he removed her sweater, his eyebrows shooting upwards as a lacy bra of midnight-blue silk was revealed.

Tiptoeing his fingertip along the delicate edging of lace, he pushed her down onto the silken rug. 'What's this?' he murmured.

'It's…a bra. What does it look like?'

'Nothing like the one you had on last night, that's for sure.' Slowly, he expelled the air from his lungs as he flattened his palm over one peaking mound. 'Did you wear it specially for me?'

Had she? She'd never worn it before. A friend had given her birthday vouchers to an upmarket lingerie shop that didn't know the meaning of words like *sensible* or *refund*. The navy set had been the most practical thing on offer, but up until today it had seemed too delicate for everyday use. There had never been a reason to wear it before, yet something had made her put it on this morning...

'Maybe subconsciously,' she admitted.

He gave a glimmer of a smile. 'A woman only wears underwear like this if she wants a man to take it off. Is that what you want me to do, Livvy? Is that what you've been longing for me to do ever since you got up this morning? To run my fingers over your beautiful pale skin and get you naked?'

She closed her eyes as his hand strayed to the bra's front clasp. She wanted to tell him that his assumption was arrogant, but how could she protest when his fingers had loosened the clip and her breasts were spilling free? The cool air hit her skin and suddenly he was bending his lips to a nipple and he was sucking on it. Nipping at it and grazing his teeth all over the sensitised nub. She gave a little squeal of pleasure and he lifted his head.

'You are very vocal in your approval, *habibi*,' he observed softly. 'Does that feel good?'

Her tongue snaked out to moisten her parched lips. 'So good,' she breathed.

'And this? Does this feel good?'

Against the rug, Livvy writhed with pleasure as his hand moved between her legs, because her body suddenly felt as if was out of her control and words seemed to be beyond her. Did he really need her to tell him that she liked the way he was sucking her nipple? The way his finger was rubbing up and down the stiff seam of her jeans at the very point where she was acutely sensitive. The finger stilled.

'Does it?' he questioned silkily.

Did he want praise? Maybe she was expected to touch *him*. To reach out to where his crotch was straining so formidably against his trousers and to trickle her fingers over his hardness. Livvy's heart began to pound. Her experience of foreplay was limited, because Rupert had known she was a virgin and had wanted to wait until they were married and had said he didn't trust himself to touch her. It wasn't until afterwards that she had discovered the reason why...

Her sex life was something she regarded as an arid area of failure, but instinct told her that Saladin Al Mektala could be the person to change all that. She suspected that what the sheikh didn't know about pleasure wouldn't be worth knowing. Yet surely it would be deceitful to let him make love to her without telling him her secret.

'Does it?' he repeated silkily, and Livvy circled her hips with frustration and guilt.

What if she told him and he rejected her—if he left her shivering and aching with frustration in front of the fire?

She had to tell him.

She stared straight into his black eyes. 'It feels incredible,' she said. 'But maybe you ought to know that I'm—'

'Driving me crazy with desire, that's for sure,' he said, moving over her to silence her words with another breathtaking kiss.

And Livvy let him. That was the shame of it. She just let him. Wrapping her arms around his neck, she kissed him back with a slow, exploratory hunger as he began to slide down the zipper of her jeans.

'Mmm…' was his only comment as he tugged the denim away to reveal the lacy blue knickers that matched her bra, before concentrating his attention on kissing her body. He whispered his lips over her breasts—his breath warm against her skin—before travelling down to her belly. She held her breath as his head travelled downwards until his dark head was positioned between her thighs. For a moment she tensed, but when he licked almost lazily at the moist panel of her panties a spasm of pleasure so intense shot through her that for a moment Livvy was scared she might faint.

Was it the half-broken cry she made in response to that intimacy that made him suddenly stop? Her nails dug hard into his shoulders in protest but he didn't appear to care.

'Don't—' she gasped.

Had he read her mind?

'Don't stop?' He looked up from his decadent position between her thighs, and smiled. 'I have no intention of stopping, but I am hungry to feel my skin next to yours, *habibi*. And while you are almost naked—I am not.'

She didn't want him to move—terrified that any movement would shatter this precarious magic—but she had little choice except to lie there and watch as he stood up and began to strip off. His shirt was silk and so were his boxers and they floated to the ground like fine gossamer. Livvy's mouth dried as his body was revealed. His dark skin glowed like richest gold and the deep shadows cast by the flickering firelight emphasised his physical perfection. A hard and rippling torso, with powerful arms and muscular legs that seemed to go on forever. Narrow hips and rock-hard buttocks. Even the powerful evidence of his arousal wasn't as daunting as it should have been because by now Livvy was alive with a need that had been buried inside her for so long that she felt she would die if he didn't make love to her.

Her heart was pounding as she stared at his erection, but when he reached down into the pocket of his trousers and drew out a condom, she felt a flutter of misgiving. Did he always carry protection with him? Did he take it for granted that there would always be a willing woman lying waiting for him like this? She thought about the women who sometimes used to accompany him to the stables—those models and actresses with their suede boots and miniskirts and real fur. For a moment she wondered how she could possibly compare to those glamorous creatures, until she forced the dark clouds of insecurity from her mind. Maybe there *was* always an accommodating female wherever he went—like a sailor having a woman in every port—but this wasn't about *convention*, was it? She'd done all that stuff and look where it had got her.

She thought about the heartache of the past and the struggle her life had been for so long. She stared over Saladin's shoulder as he slithered her panties off and moved over her. Outside the world was white and still and silent, apart from the distant ticking of a clock. Time was passing, but they were completely alone and this moment would never come again. And she had to seize it—to grab it—and to hell with the consequences.

Yet once before she had blinded herself to the truth. She'd buried her head in the sand and allowed herself to be treated like a fool by the man she'd been engaged to. Was she going to repeat that pattern of behaviour all her life—to run away from what she was afraid to face?

'Saladin,' she whispered as he rubbed his thumb over her clitoris. 'There's something you should know.'

'The only thing I need to know is whether you like… this…'

She closed her eyes. *Like* it? She imagined that even a marble statue would have squirmed beneath his questing finger, but that wasn't the point. The words came out in a bald rush—but what other way was there to say them? 'I'm a virgin.'

His fingers—which had been working rhythmically against her heated flesh—now stilled. He raised his head to look at her, his eyes full of disbelief—but there was something else in their depths, too. Something she didn't recognise. Something dark and tortured. Something that scared her.

'Is this some sort of joke?' he demanded in a strangled kind of voice.

Wondering what had made him look so *bleak*, Livvy shook her head. 'It's no joke,' she said. 'Why would I joke about something like that? It's the truth. I might not be very proud of it—but it's the truth.'

He rolled away from her and she noticed that his erection had diminished. 'How can this be?' he bit out. 'You are nearly thirty years old. You were engaged to be married. I know what Western women are like. They lose their innocence early and they take many lovers!'

His crass generalisations dispelled some of her insecurity and made Livvy start to claw back some dignity—something that wasn't particularly easy when she wasn't wearing any clothes. Did she dare walk over to the sofa where the soft woollen throw she kept for

cold winter nights was folded? Too right she did—
because staying here completely naked was making
her feel even more vulnerable than she already did. On
shaky legs she rose to stand, aware of his heated gaze
following her as she walked over to get the blanket and
brought it back to the fireside. But as she wrapped it
around herself and sat at the other end of the rug, she
became aware that his erection was back. And how.
Hastily averting her eyes, she turned to throw a log
into the neglected fire.

'I hate to ruin your prejudices, but not all women
conform to the stereotypes you've just described,' she
said. 'The law of averages suggests that there will be
some older virgins as well as young ones.'

Saladin's mouth thinned with displeasure, thinking
that there couldn't have been a more inappropriate moment for her to try to dazzle him with statistics, and
he was amazed she should even dare try. He felt the
heavy throb of his heart. He had wanted sex. Simple,
uncomplicated sex with a willing woman. He didn't
want someone with *issues* or *baggage*. He didn't want
someone who, with her purity, had stirred up memories he had locked away a long time ago. For he had
only ever slept with one virgin before, and that virgin
had been his beautiful wife. Pain and guilt clenched
at his heart as he stared at her.

'I don't understand,' he said coldly.

'You don't have to. I'm…' And suddenly he saw the
uncertainty that flickered across her pale and freckled
face. 'I'm sorry if I led you on.'

An unwanted but persistent point of principle made
him shake his head. 'We led each other on,' he said

heavily. 'But it is true that you have left it a little *late* to drop this particular bombshell.'

Awkwardly, she shrugged. 'Do you want to get dressed?'

Saladin shook his head. What he wanted was to be back where he'd been less than five minutes ago, not stuck in the middle of some damned conversation! 'I don't believe it,' he breathed. 'I thought it was the custom in the West to have sex before marriage—and you were on the very brink of marriage. So what happened?'

'It's difficult to put into words.'

'You don't seem to have had much problem with words so far.'

She shifted uncomfortably beneath his gaze. 'I think I was born in the wrong age,' she said slowly. 'I was a tomboy who loved messing around in the countryside. I climbed trees and used to make dens with the boys from the village. I never had posters of pop stars on my walls like all the other girls in my class. I was more interested in horses—horses were my life. In fact, everything was just like one of those old-fashioned children's stories, until my mum died.'

'That must have been hard,' he said.

She shrugged again and suddenly he thought she looked much younger than nearly thirty.

'Lots of children lose their mothers,' she said. 'But not so many have a father who was left feeling very vulnerable. A rich widower who became perfect marriage fodder for the kind of woman commonly known as a gold-digger.'

'I have some experience of that breed myself,' he observed wryly. 'So what happened?'

She shrugged. 'He fell for a busty blonde with a penchant for diamonds and couture and then he married her. My father was a country gentleman and this house had been in his family for generations, but his new wife preferred luxury travel and sailing in sunny waters on a lavish yacht. She was the kind of woman who would buy an entire new wardrobe before every trip—and we weren't the sort of family who had a lot of ready cash. Most of it was tied up in the house. Would you…?' Again, she licked her lips. 'Would you like a blanket, or something?'

He would like *something*, but he suspected he wasn't going to get it right then. 'Why, is my nakedness bothering you?'

'A little.'

'Just a little?' He let his gaze slide down to his groin before raising his eyes to her flaming cheeks. 'I must be slipping. Very well, bring me a blanket if it makes you feel better.'

He wondered if she was aware that he was being treated to a tantalising glimpse of her bare bottom as she walked over to a second sofa and grabbed another blanket, though he noticed that she averted her gaze again as she thrust it at him before resuming her position at the other end of the rug.

'So what happened?' he questioned, watching as she huddled herself in a cocoon of soft wool. 'Or can I guess? Did she grow bored with marriage to an older man? Did she demand more and more money, until she'd bled him dry?'

Her eyes widened. 'How did you know?'

'Because I know what women are like,' he said. 'And your stepmother was conforming to a pattern that isn't exactly ground-breaking.' His eyes narrowed. 'And ironically, you met your own male version of the gold-digger in de Vries.'

She nodded before staring down at the pattern on the rug as if completely absorbed by it, but when she lifted her face he noted that her expression was calm—as if she had practised very hard to look that way.

'That's right. I can't believe that I didn't see it for myself, my only defence being that I was very young,' she said. 'His stables were in trouble—everyone knew that—but nobody realised quite how bad the problem was. He knew I was an only child and he saw this house and made the assumption we were rolling in money. Which, of course, we weren't. My father was quite an old man by then and he was ill. We had a lot of carers who were coming in and helping me look after him, and they cost an absolute fortune.'

'And I suppose that was also occupying a lot of your time and energy?' he said grimly.

She nodded again. 'He was very frail by then, and Rupert seemed so understanding about it all. He didn't seem to mind when I had to cancel dinner because one of the carers hadn't shown up. And because he was my first real boyfriend, I had nothing to compare him with. I just thought he was being kind. When he said…' She sucked in a deep breath. 'When he said that he wanted to wait until we were married before we had sex, I found that somehow reassuring.'

Saladin nodded. Yes, he could see that. A horse-mad, motherless tomboy whose only role models had been an old man who should have known better and an avaricious stepmother who was out for all she could get. No wonder Livvy hadn't known the rules about relationships, or men, or sex. Nobody had bothered to explain them to her, had they?

'Don't you realise that it reflects badly on him, not you?' he questioned savagely. 'That a man who dumps a woman on her wedding day because she has less money than he thought is not a *real* man. We have a name for that kind of man in Jazratan, but I will not sully your ears with it.'

'But it wasn't just the money. There was something else.' She twisted some of the blanket's tassels between her fingers. 'It turned out that he was sleeping with one of the female grooms and had been for some time, which was why he hadn't tried harder to get into bed with me. Not just any groom, either—but my best friend. And there was me thinking that he was displaying old-fashioned values of chivalry designed to win a woman's heart, not realising that I was being betrayed by the two people I considered closest to me.' She gave a short and bitter laugh. 'What a fool I was.'

'You shouldn't beat yourself up for wanting to believe the best in people,' he said, his voice growing hard. 'Though I hope you've learned your lesson now. It's always better to think the worst. That way you don't get disappointed.'

She stared at him. 'You've been very...' Her voice tailed off.

'Very what?'

'It doesn't matter.'

'I think it does.'

'*Understanding.*' She gave an embarrassed kind of shrug.

'What did you think I was going to do?' he questioned roughly. 'Carry on as if nothing had happened—

kiss away your protests and ignore your obvious reservations? Or maybe you *wanted* me to fulfil the fantasy of the exotic stranger who ravishes the willing but innocent woman. Who takes away the responsibility so you didn't have to make the decision for yourself. Is that what you would have liked? It's a common enough fantasy, especially where desert sheikhs are concerned. Would that have made it easier for you, Livvy?'

She licked her lips. 'I wasn't even going to tell you.'

'No, I gathered that,' he said drily. 'So what changed your mind?'

She shrugged again and the blanket slipped down over her shoulders, before she hauled it back up again. 'I thought it was dishonest not to. I thought you might be one of those men for whom virginity is a big deal.'

Saladin was silent as he considered her words. Was it? Her eyes were wide as she looked at him and he could read the faint anxiety in their depths. He supposed it was. For a man in his position, virginity was an essential requirement of any future queen. But he was not looking for a queen. He had been there, done that. What was it they said in the West? Bought the T-shirt.

His mouth hardened as she held his gaze with those startling amber eyes. Was she seeking reassurance? Holding out for an impossible dream? He felt the hard throb of desire at his groin and shifted his weight. This was a unique situation, but despite his undeniable lust—lust was interchangeable, because there was always another female eager enough to open her legs for him. If it were anyone else, he would get dressed, make a quick phone call and get the hell out of there— no matter how many damned snow ploughs it took.

And that was what he *should* do—he knew that. Because purity was something he always associated with just one woman—and wouldn't it dishonour Alya's memory if he were to take the innocence of another? Every instinct he possessed—except for the sexual instinct—told him to leave now and get away while he still could.

But Livvy Miller still had something he wanted. Something that only she could provide. And maybe he had something *she* wanted, because surely she didn't want to carry on like this. Was now the time for a little adult negotiation? If he fulfilled a need in her—then wouldn't she feel morally obliged to do the same for him?

On her face he could read trepidation warring with desire, and a genuine sense of injustice washed over him. How crazy was it that she had never known the joy of sex? That a woman who was known for her physicality and skill on a horse should have neglected her own body for so long?

He didn't move—he didn't dare—because it was vital he didn't influence her decision, even though he knew that another kiss and she would be melting beneath him. But it had to be *her* decision, not his. His gaze was unwavering as he looked at her.

'So,' he questioned silkily. 'Do you want me to take your virginity, Livvy?'

CHAPTER SEVEN

LIVVY DIDN'T ANSWER straight away. It seemed like
something out of a dream—the powerful sheikh asking if she wanted him to take her virginity, with all the
impartiality of someone enquiring whether she'd like
a spoonful of sugar in her coffee.

As she stared into the provocative gleam of Saladin's black eyes, she thought about everything that had
brought her to this moment. The public shame of being
jilted that had hit her so hard, even though she'd done
her best to hold her head up high afterwards. She'd
walked away from the world of horses without a backward glance and had started a new life.

Out of a sense of loyalty to her father's memory
and a determination that Rupert's rejection wouldn't
destroy her completely, she'd done her best to keep
Wightwick Manor going. On a shoestring budget she'd
worked hard to make her bed and breakfast business a
success. But now she could see that she had neglected
her own needs in the process. She'd put her emotional
life on a back burner, letting her twenties trickle away
beneath the hard work of maintaining an old house like
this. She hadn't done dates or parties or make-up—
she'd spent any spare money on roof tiles, or getting the

windows painted. She hadn't gone off for minibreaks or enjoyed sunny vacations with girlfriends, drinking lurid-coloured cocktails while they were chatted up by waiters. She hadn't even tried to find herself a new boyfriend. She'd told herself she didn't need the potential pain of another relationship.

Yet here she was—naked underneath a blanket while a similarly naked Saladin surveyed her from the other end of the rug. She stared into the dark smoulder of his eyes and wondered how best to respond to his question. She supposed she could say no. Act prim and outraged—and tell him that she wasn't interested in giving her virginity to him, like some kind of medieval sacrifice. He was certainly sophisticated enough to take it on the chin. She doubted he would feel more than a moment of regret, and she would probably be knocked down by the rush of women eager to take her place.

But it wasn't quite that straightforward, because she still wanted him. He'd kissed her passionately and made her feel she was part of something magical. He'd made her feel things she didn't think she was capable of feeling—a powerful passion that had overwhelmed her and a need that had flooded hotly through her veins. He'd set her body on *fire*. She thought about the way he'd touched her—whispering his mouth over each breast in turn, grazing them with his teeth and making her urge him on with writhing hips. She remembered the way his head had slid down between her thighs and something molten and sweet had begun to tug at the very core of her—something that was making refusal seem like a crazy idea. And she knew something else—that she would never get another chance like this.

Desert sheikhs promising untold pleasure didn't come along more than once in a lifetime.

She stared at him.

'Yes,' she said, in a low voice. 'Yes, I want you to take my virginity.'

His face showed no immediate reaction. The hawk-like features displayed no hint of triumph although his lips curved in the briefest of smiles.

'Come here,' he instructed softly.

She wondered briefly why he couldn't come to *her*, but his words were compelling and masterful and Livvy stood up and began to walk towards him, clutching the blanket against her skin like a makeshift dress. She could feel his eyes burning into her—as if that piercing black gaze was capable of scorching through the wool to the body beneath. Her footsteps faltered as she reached him, uncertain about what to do next, but he reached out and slid his thumb over her ankle, massaging briefly against the jut of bone there, before beginning to stroke his way up her calf. Livvy swallowed as pleasure began to ripple over her skin. It seemed such a light, innocuous movement to such an innocent part of the body and yet…yet…

'Saladin,' she whispered.

'Shh.'

The back of her knee was next—a tiny circular movement that must have made her loosen her grip on the blanket because he gave it a single tug and it slid to the ground, leaving her standing naked in front of him. Automatically, her hands flew up to conceal her breasts, before he shook his head.

'Do not cover yourself, Livvy,' he instructed softly. 'Your body is very beautiful. It is small and neat, yet strong and supple. It pleases me very much and I wish to look at it.'

She kept her hands exactly where they were, even though his words were making her nipples peak against her fingers. 'You're making me feel like an object.'

'Not an object,' he demurred, reaching up and pulling her down into his arms, so that her flesh met the comforting warmth of his. He pushed the mussed hair away from her face and used the edge of his thumb to trace the outline of her lips. 'Not even a subject, since I do not rule over you. So stop looking at me with those anxious eyes and relax, because I am going to give you pleasure such as you have never dreamed of.'

'But I don't have a clue what to do,' she whispered.

'And that,' he said unevenly, 'is part of your attraction.'

Only part of it, she wondered dazedly as his mouth came down towards her. What was the other part?

But his kiss was powerful enough to send any last doubts skittering from her mind, and the slow caress of his lips made further deliberations impossible. All she could think about was what he was doing. He was holding her close—so close—making her feel as if every cell in her body were sensitive to each seeking caress.

At first his touch wasn't overtly sexual. The hands that were cupping her face seemed more interested in exploring the thickness of her hair and the outline of her face. And when that innocent exploration made her relax, he started stroking his hands down the sides of her body—until she was moving restlessly against him.

He must have known that her impatience was growing, but he paid no attention to her squirming movements. He just took his time—drawing out the exquisite torture as his fingers slowly acquainted themselves with her skin. Inch by tantalising inch, he touched her. First her breasts and then her ribcage and the undulation of her waist. She held her breath as he turned his attention to her belly and teased her by brushing his fingers farther down to delve inside the soft fuzz of hair. Yet his hawklike features remained impassive even though she could feel the tension building in his powerful body. She could sense his restraint—as if he was battling his own desire in order to feed hers.

'Saladin,' she breathed, looking into his eyes to find herself ensnared by a smoky black gaze.

'Want me?' His thumb brushed against the moist and engorged bud hidden by the soft curls, and she let out a little murmur of assent as she nodded.

'I…I think so.'

'I think so, too,' he said, his voice suddenly growing harsh.

He moved over her, his hardness nudging against her wet heat as she opened her legs for him with an instinct that seemed to come from somewhere deep inside her. She became aware of so many things—his weight and his strength and the subtle scent of sandalwood and salt that clung to his skin.

'Look at me,' he urged softly.

Until he spoke, she hadn't even realised her eyes had closed again. She let the lids flutter open to meet his heated gaze as he made that first thrust deep inside her—a long, slow thrust that made her gasp and instantly he stilled, his eyes narrowing.

'It hurts?'

Breathlessly, she shook her head. 'Not really. It just feels…'

'What?'

'Big.'

Saladin smiled—he couldn't help himself. But her unintentional boost to his masculine ego only increased his hunger—if that was possible—and it was a moment before he could trust himself to move again. Already he felt close to a tipping point that had been reached the moment he had entered her. He could feel her flesh enclosing him as sweetly as an oyster clamped its shell around the glistening pearl. She was so tight. So wet. So...*unexpected*. But he reined back his sudden urgent desire to ride her as fiercely as he would ride one of his horses. Because this was her first time, he reminded himself. This was the touchstone by which she would measure all the men who would follow. And he must make it a good experience—the very best experience—for all kinds of reasons.

So he concentrated on kissing and fondling her. On doing all the things that women liked best and on holding back his own desire. And even though his sexual hunger was at a high that was almost unendurable, it felt exquisite. Maybe because it was the first time in a long time that he had put a woman's needs before his own. Usually he didn't have to, because he prided himself on being able to make a woman orgasm within moments of touching her, but this was different. Virgins were different...

The pain of memory shot through him like a dark streak of lightning and for a moment he screwed his eyes tightly shut, cursing the thoughts that crowded into his mind—and slamming down the barriers before they could take root there.

He drew in a deep breath and began to objectify

what was happening, in order to distract himself. He concentrated on Livvy's reaction rather than his own—watching as her eyes grew dark and her cheeks flushed. He felt the tension in her fingers as they kneaded against his sweat-sheened back. He could feel the urgency in her thighs, which were digging hard against his hips, and the way she instinctively angled her pelvis to encourage him to go deeper. He tipped his head back as she covered his shoulder with a flurry of frantic little kisses that seemed to grow in crescendo as he drove her towards her climax.

He knew when she was about to come. He could sense the change in her body—the unmistakable quiver of expectation and excitement edged with the sense of disbelief that heralded any orgasm. And that was when he kissed her again. Gripped her hips hard as he drove into her. Imprisoned her against his exquisitely aroused length as her back began to arch and he waited for the split second of stillness before she started spasming against his flesh. He thought she called out his name as he gave into his own release, which he could hold back no longer—his own pleasure increased by the sensation of her still quivering helplessly in his arms.

It took him a long time to come down and, unusually, he stayed where he was for a long time—withdrawing only when he felt the returning stir of an erection. He rolled away from her, pulling the discarded blanket over her, unable to resist a glance at her flushed face and the bright, honey-coloured eyes, before her eyelids fluttered sleepily down. But for once he did not want sleep—something his body habitually demanded after sex, which helped emphasise the distance he craved and lessened the chances of being asked pointless questions about the possibility of a long-term relationship.

For once he was wide awake and more alive than he could remember feeling in a long, long time. He wanted to hear what the feisty little redhead had to say about her first experience of sex, although he told himself that his interest was simply academic. He was not looking for praise because he knew how good he was—but he needed her to be satisfied with what had just happened. *He needed to keep her sweet.*

Stroking a slow finger over one flushed breast, he smiled. 'No need to ask whether you enjoyed that.'

His murmured words dissolved the clouds of contentment that had settled on her and, with an effort, Livvy blinked herself awake. Her eyes felt so heavy, it was as if someone had crept in and placed two tiny pebbles on them while she hadn't been looking. She met Saladin's dark gaze. His skin was flushed and his eyes were smoky, yet he sounded more concerned with his own performance rating than with anything else. She told herself that his arrogance didn't matter because nothing had felt this good in a long time— maybe ever—and she'd be a fool not to hold on to it while she could. She felt…warm. Complete. As if she were floating on a pink cloud that she never wanted to get off.

She studied his hawklike features and sensual lips and she wanted him all over again. All she had to do was to lean forward to kiss him, and she had to fight the longing to do just that because something warned her to tread carefully. She needed to remember that the sheikh was unlike other men—and her own track record was hopeless. She didn't want to make a fool of herself and, more important, she didn't want to give him the opportunity to reject her. Because hadn't she vowed that she would never get rejected for a second time?

She must not make the mistake of falling in love with him.

What would such a seasoned lover as Saladin normally require in such circumstances? she wondered, and something told her to play it straight. Just because her system was flooded with hormones that were making her want to do inappropriate things like stroke his face and be all *tender*—didn't mean she was going to listen to them.

'I don't think you'd need me to be wired up to a machine to register my heart-rate to realise that it was a very satisfying experience,' she said.

He looked surprised, there was no denying that—and neither could she deny the little rush of pleasure that gave her.

'So you don't regret it?'

Livvy chewed on her lip. Did she? She thought about the vow she had made to herself a long time ago.

'I don't do regrets,' she said quietly. 'Not anymore.'

Saladin's eyes narrowed. It was not the glowing endorsement he had expected, nor the compliancy of a woman who was eager for more. If he had been on territory he could call his own—a hotel suite, perhaps—then he might have taken himself off for a long shower and left her lying there to think about the wisdom of her words. But he wasn't. He was in *her* house on *her* rug—and she was still in possession of something he wanted. He gave a slow smile as he drew a thoughtful finger down over her breast and felt her shiver. Did she really think she would be able to deny him now that she had tasted the pleasure he could give her?

'I'm going to make love to you again,' he said.

But instead of being captured by his gaze, she was looking across the room at a radiating blue-white light.

'Your phone's vibrating,' she said.

And her damned *cat* chose that precise moment to stalk into the room and hiss at him.

CHAPTER EIGHT

Livvy watched as Saladin walked across the room to answer his phone, not seeming to care that away from the fierce blaze of the fire the unheated room was icy cold on his naked body. Or maybe his careless, almost sauntering journey was deliberate. Perhaps he thought that the sight of him without any clothes would set her heart racing and cast some kind of erotic spell on her. And if that was the case, he was right.

Beside her Peppa gave a plaintive meow, but for once Livvy's stroking of the cat's abundant fur was distracted, because how could she concentrate on anything other than the sight of the magnificent sheikh?

She found herself watching him hungrily in the way that Peppa sometimes watched a beautiful bird as it hopped around the garden. The powerful shafts of his thighs rose to greet the paler globes of buttocks, leading to the narrow taper of his hips and waist. Livvy swallowed. The proud way he held his head and broad line of his shoulders reminded her of a statue she'd once seen in a museum. It seemed impossible that moments before he'd been deep inside her, making her cry out with pleasure.

A man she barely knew—yet one who ironically

knew her more intimately than anyone. She'd told him about still being a virgin and then, very slowly—he had made love to her.

She wrapped the blanket round her as he picked up the vibrating phone and, after clicking the connection, began speaking rapidly in an unknown language she assumed was his native tongue. She noticed that he listened for some—not much—of the time, but mostly he seemed to be barking out commands. She gave a wry smile as she lay back on the rug. She guessed that was what sheikhs did.

Resting her head against her folded arms, she waited—her newfound sense of torpor making her aware of her glowing skin and her sense of satisfaction. And Saladin was responsible for that. For all his arrogance and sense of entitlement, he had proved the most considerate and exciting first lover a woman could wish for.

Lazily, she turned her head and looked out of the window. The snow had stopped falling but there were no signs of a thaw. The landscape looked as pretty as a Christmas card—unreal and somehow impenetrable, as if they were in their own private little bubble and nobody else could get in. Inside, the lack of electricity was beginning to bite and it was starting to get cold. The decorated tree looked strange without the rainbow glow of fairy lights, and despite the blaze of the fire the room had taken a distinct drop in temperature. She dreaded to think how icy it must be upstairs. Some of her euphoria began to leave her as Livvy started to consider the more practical concerns of the power cut. Eight guests were due to arrive the day after tomorrow and she had no electricity!

Her torpor forgotten, she jumped up and grabbed the silky knickers that were lying in a heap on the floor, and had just slithered them on when she felt a light but proprietorial hand on her bottom.

'What do you think you're doing?'

She turned round and steeled herself against the glint of displeasure in Saladin's dark eyes.

'I'm getting dressed.'

'Why?' With possessive intimacy, he trailed his finger down over the silk-covered crack between her buttocks. 'When I want to make love to you again.'

'Because…' Furious at the way her concerns about the electricity should have morphed into concerns about the very different kind of electricity that was sparking from her skin where he touched her, Livvy tried to pull away. 'Because there's no power and my freezer will be defrosting, and the roads might be cleared at any time. And there are eight guests who will be arriving for Christmas who won't have any croissants for breakfast if the freezer defrosts!' She drew in a deep breath. 'And while these might not be the kind of problems that would normally enter your radar, this is the *real world*, Saladin—and it's a world in which I have to live!'

'And how does getting dressed solve anything when your guests aren't due today?'

She met the mocking expression in his eyes. *It stops me from getting too close to you again. It stops me from feeling any more vulnerable than I'm currently feeling.*

Livvy never knew how she would have answered his question because suddenly the electricity came on in a flurry of light and sound. The tree lights blazed into life and three small lamps began to glow. Somewhere in another part of the house a distant radio began playing and Peppa jumped to her feet and gave a growling little purr.

'The power's back on,' he said.

'Yes,' she answered, in a strange flat voice.

And then the landline started to ring—its piercing sound shattering the silence of their haven. Livvy stared at Saladin, aware of a sinking sensation that felt awfully like disappointment. The outside world was about to intrude and, right then, she didn't want it to.

'Better answer it,' he said.

Clad in just her knickers, Livvy scooted across the room to pick up the phone and nodded her head as she listened to the voice on the other end.

'No, no. That's quite all right, Alison,' she said, aware that Saladin was putting a guard in front of the fire. 'Honestly, it really doesn't matter. I quite understand. I would have done exactly the same in your position. Yes. Yes, I hope so. Okay. I will. Yes. Of course. And a merry Christmas to you, too. Goodbye.'

Slowly, she replaced the receiver as Saladin straightened up and suddenly a part of his anatomy was looking like no museum statue *she'd* ever seen, and it was all still so new to her that she didn't know whether it was rude to stare—even though she was finding it very difficult *not* to stare.

'Who was it?' he questioned and Livvy wondered whether she'd imagined that faint note of amusement in his voice, as if he was perfectly aware of her dilemma.

She shrugged. 'My guests. Someone called Alison Clark who was due to arrive with a load of her polo friends. They rang to say that the weather forecast is too dodgy and they're not coming after all. They've decided to spend Christmas at some fancy hotel in London instead.'

'And are you disappointed?' he questioned smoothly.

'I don't know if *disappointed* is the word I'd use,' she said, aware that a long and empty Christmas now loomed ahead of her. And wasn't that one of the reasons why she always stayed open during the holiday? Because being busy meant she didn't have to look at all the things that were missing in her own life. 'It means I won't get paid, of course.'

There was a pause as he glittered her a smile. 'But that is where you are wrong, Livvy,' he said softly. 'Don't you see that fate has played right into our hands? You are now free to take up my offer and return to Jazratan with me. You can forget about niggling domestic duties over the holidays and use your neglected healing powers on my horse, for which I will reward you handsomely.'

The sum he mentioned was so large that for a moment Livvy thought he was joking, and for a moment she was seriously tempted. Yet some stubborn sense of pride made her shake her head. 'That's far too much.'

He raised his eyebrows. 'First time I've ever heard anyone complain about being paid too much.'

'It should be a fair price,' she persisted stubbornly. 'Not one that sounds like winning the national lottery.'

'What is fair is what I am prepared to pay for your services,' he argued. 'If your gift was more widely distributed, then obviously the price would be a lot lower. But it isn't, and what you have is rare, Livvy—we both know that.'

She knew what he was doing. He was manipulating

her and he was doing it very effectively. He was making her an offer too good to refuse and she was scared. Scared to try. Scared of failing. Scared of his reaction if she *did* fail. And scared of so much else besides.

'But what if this so-called *gift* no longer exists?' she said. 'There's no guarantee that my intervention will work. Burkaan may not respond to my treatment, we both know that.'

'Yes, I know that,' he said. 'But at least I will have tried. I will have done all that is in my power to help my horse.'

She wasn't imagining the sudden hollowness in his voice, or the accompanying bleakness in his eyes, and it was that that made up Livvy's mind for her. Yes, Saladin Al Mektala had the kind of unimaginable riches and influence that other people could only dream of, but when it boiled down to it he was just a man who was desperate to save his beloved horse.

'Very well.' She bent down and picked up her bra. 'I'll come to Jazratan with you.'

'Now what are you doing?'

She straightened up. 'I'm getting dressed, of course. There's a lot I have to sort out. I need to organise someone to feed the cat, for a start.'

'I'm sure you do, but there is something of much greater urgency.' His voice had grown silky. 'And don't look at me with those big honey-coloured eyes and pretend you don't know what I'm talking about.'

Taking the bra from her unprotesting fingers, he dropped it to the floor and wrapped his arms around her waist, securing her to the spot, so that he could kiss her. And once he had started kissing her, she was hungry for more. She rose up on tiptoe to curl her hands possessively around his neck and he gave a low laugh of triumph.

But this time he didn't push her to the rug and slowly thrust himself inside her. Instead, he bent and slid his arm underneath her knees, lifting her up so that she was cradled effortlessly in front of his chest.

'Where are you taking me?' she whispered as he headed for the door.

'To bed.'

She looked up at him. 'Why?'

'Are you serious? You know exactly why. Because I want sex with you again, and once on a hard floor is quite enough when there is the promise of a soft mattress.'

'Actually, my mattress happens to be very firm.'

'That's good.' He slid his hand over her bottom and gave it a squeeze. 'I like firm.'

Her cheeks hot with embarrassment and excitement, Livvy turned her face into his chest. He was taking control and she was letting him. *I want sex with you again*, he'd said—in a way that could almost be described as abrupt. There were no euphemisms tripping off his tongue, were there? No tender words of affection to feed her romantic fantasies. *He's being truthful*, she reminded herself. *He's telling it as it is.*

Yet it was difficult to keep fantasy totally at bay when a naked sheikh was in the process of kicking open her bedroom door and depositing her on her bed.

'Now,' he said as he straddled her, his fingers hooking into the soft silk of her knickers.

She thought he was about to slide them down as he'd done before, but the sudden sound of delicate fabric being ripped made her eyes widen in astonishment and, yes, in excitement, too.

'I can't…' Her heart began to hammer against her ribcage. 'I can't believe you just did that.'

'Well, I did—and here's the proof,' he drawled, dangling the tattered fragments from his index finger like a trophy.

'Those are my best knickers,' she protested.

'Were,' he corrected. 'But they were an obstruction to my desire, and I don't do obstruction. Ever. You shouldn't have put them back on, Livvy.'

'That is…outrageous,' she spluttered.

'Perhaps it is,' he agreed unsteadily. 'But you like me being outrageous, don't you, *habibi*? You like the sense that I am now free to do this…' With a light and teasing movement, he began to brush his finger over her searing heat. Back and forth it went in a relentless rhythm so delicious that she almost leaped off the bed.

'Oh,' she breathed.

'And, of course, I shall make sure you have new panties,' he said unsteadily.

She felt his warm breath heating her face as he lowered his lips towards her. 'What, just so that you can rip them off again?' she managed indistinctly.

'Of course. Because I think we're both discovering what we like. You like me being masterful, don't you, my beauty?' His finger was continuing with its insistent, stroking movement. 'Which is very convenient, since being masterful comes very easily to me.'

Livvy was so aroused by this stage that she barely noticed he must have been in possession of another condom all the while he'd been carrying her upstairs, because he was now stroking it on with practised fingers and easing himself inside her, and she gasped—her cry catching in her throat like a crumb. But this time there was nothing but glorious anticipation coursing around her veins like thick, sweet honey as he entered her. Because this time she knew what was coming.

'Oh, Saladin,' she said, the tender words tumbling out of her mouth—driven by her sheer delight in the moment and wanting him to know how special this felt. 'You are…'

But her breathless words died on her lips as she felt him tense inside her, as if she'd wronged him in some way. She looked up to see that his face had become a mask—stony and forbidding.

'Don't say soft words to me, because I don't want to hear them,' he instructed harshly. 'I don't do tenderness, Livvy. Do you understand?'

'S-sure,' she said uncertainly, and closed her eyes so he wouldn't see her hurt and confusion.

But something had changed—although maybe it was just her own perception of what was happening. He seemed like a man on a mission. As if he was intent on demonstrating his sexual superiority—or demonstrating *something*. Why else did he seem to set about showcasing how many times he could have her orgasm? Of having her plead with him not to stop? Over and over again he made love to her in different ways, as if he intended to make up for all the sex she'd missed out on in her twenty-nine years. Or was it all about power? About showing her who was really the boss?

CHAPTER NINE

SALADIN HEARD THE whir of helicopter blades long before the craft entered the immediate airspace of the house. Moving his wrist carefully so as not to wake Livvy, he glanced at his watch and gave a small nod of satisfaction. Exactly on time and exactly as he had instructed.

He glanced over at the head that was lying next to him—Livvy's bright hair spread out over the pillow. Her lips were parted as she breathed and there was a rosy flush on her freckled cheeks. He felt another stir of desire and contemplated moving his fingertip down over one silken thigh as he thought back to the previous night and most of the subsequent day that he'd spent in her bed. They had taken short breaks for food and for a shared and very erotic shower, and at one point they'd even scrambled into their clothes and gone out tramping through the snowy countryside. But for the most part they had been shut in her bedroom, making love so often that he should have been exhausted, when all he felt was a delicious kind of high.

Because Olivia Miller had proved an exciting lover—more exciting than she should have been, given her lack of experience. Her light, strong body had bent beneath his with the suppleness of a young sapling as he'd driven into her over and over again. She had embraced sex with a passion and athleticism that had taken his sometimes jaded breath away. And if at one point she had made the mistake of going all tender on him, it was a mistake she would not be repeating, for he had warned her off starting to care for him—and royal protocol would ensure that the message was slammed home to her. For this was the last time they would lie together like this...

He felt a stir of something else and acknowledged the uncomfortable stab of his conscience, knowing he had manipulated her in a particularly ruthless fashion. He had taken her virginity because it seemed wrong that a relatively young woman should be living such a celibate existence. And because he had wanted her very badly. But there had been another reason why he had made love to her...knowing that a woman rarely refused a man something if he gave her enough pleasure. And it had worked, hadn't it? She would now be accompanying him to his homeland, as he had intended she would all along.

He felt another stab of conscience. His own doubts hadn't stayed around for long, had they? His guilt about taking her virginity and the symbolic betrayal of his wife hadn't lasted beyond that first, sweet thrust.

He felt the returning throb of an erection and wondered if there was time for another swift coupling prior to their flight before deciding against it. She was going to need to wash and brush up before the trip to his homeland, and he was going to have to deal with his advisors and bodyguards who would doubtless be angry about this solo trip, though they would never dare show

it. And although they would invariably guess that he
had been doing more than taking tea with the fiery-
headed horse expert, there was no need to flaunt his
affairs openly in front of such a notoriously conserva-
tive group of men. And besides, this would be the end
of it. His conscience would trouble him no longer, for
there would be no sexual relationship once they were
in Jazratan. His mouth hardened. He never brought his
lovers to his homeland for reasons that were practical
and reasons that were painful.

The clatter of the helicopter blades interrupted his
introspection and, gently, he shook Livvy awake. Her
lashes fluttered open and he could see the momentary confusion that clouded her amber eyes as she
looked around and realised she was naked in bed with
him.

Much less shy than after their first encounter, she
sat up, the duvet tumbling to her waist and highlight-
ing the pert thrust of her breasts, and Saladin cursed
the powerful wave of desire that shot through him.

'What's that noise?'

'My helicopter.'

She blinked at him. 'It's *here*?'

'It's about to land.'

'It's dark outside,' she said sleepily.

'That's because we've been in bed most of the day
and it's late. You'll need to get showered, changed and
packed,' he added. 'Because we have to leave—and as
quickly as possible.'

Livvy felt disorientated as she brushed her untidy
hair away from her face and wondered why Saladin
was suddenly being so cool towards her. Because she'd
obeyed his curt instructions to the letter, hadn't she?

She certainly hadn't been in any way tender towards him after he'd warned her off. She'd responded to his lovemaking with nothing more controversial than a newfound passion and enjoyment. She waited for him to touch her again—or to kiss her, or *something*—but he was already picking up his cell phone and tapping out a number, and she told herself not to make a big deal out of it. Because hadn't she been firm in her resolve last night that she wasn't going to do anything stupid like falling in love with him?

Sliding out of bed, she went along the corridor to the shower, grateful that the boiler was working again and there was plenty of hot water. She remembered the shower they'd shared some time after lunch, and her cheeks burned as she tipped shampoo into the palm of her hand and relived the memory of what had happened.

Because despite his emotional detachment, it had been amazing. Every single second of it. Better than she'd ever imagined, even in her wildest dreams. Suddenly she was *glad* that Rupert had never consummated their relationship. Glad that it had been Saladin who had been her first lover, because instinct told her that no other man could make her feel the way the desert sheikh had done.

She tried to envisage someone other than Saladin touching her, but the thought of another man's hands on her body made her stomach clench with distaste. She turned her face towards the hot jets of water, knowing she mustn't read anything into what had just happened, because that would be setting herself up to be a victim. And hadn't she sworn she would never be a victim again? It was sex, that was all. Nothing but sex—

beautiful and empowering, but ultimately meaningless. So why not just enjoy it while she could?

Back in her bedroom, she stuffed her ripped panties into the bin, dressed in jeans and a sweater and then found her old jodhpurs at the back of the wardrobe and began packing a suitcase. Layering in casual clothes and T-shirts plus a couple of smarter dresses, she went over to the bookcase and picked out a couple of long-neglected books. By the time she got downstairs, the helicopter had landed on the back field and Saladin was standing beside the Christmas tree, still talking into his cell phone.

He cut the connection immediately, but his eyes didn't seem particularly warm as he turned to look at her, and he made no attempt to touch her as she walked over to him. There was no lingering kiss acknowledging their shared intimacy. No arm placed casually around her shoulder. Anyone observing them would have assumed that they were simply boss and employee, not two people who, a short time ago, had been writhing around in ecstasy together upstairs.

Boss and employee.

Which was exactly what they were.

'Your hair is still wet,' he observed. 'You'll get cold.'

Trying to ignore his critical stare, Livvy forced a smile. 'I have a woolly hat I can wear.'

'As you wish.' He glanced around. 'Do you need to lock up the house?'

'No, I thought I'd leave the doors open to see if any seasonal burglar fancies taking their chances,' she replied sarcastically. 'Of course I need to lock the house up!'

She wanted him to stop talking to her as if he were a robot and to kiss her again. To convince her that what had happened last night hadn't been some crazy kind of dream that was fading by the second.

But he didn't. He seemed suddenly *distant*. As if he had retreated behind an invisible barrier she couldn't access. Instead of being her cajoling and vital lover, he had effortlessly morphed into his real role of lofty and exalted sheikh.

Like a scene from an adventure movie, she found herself following him across the dark and snowy grass towards the helicopter, beside which stood a couple of burly men who bowed deeply before the sheikh before speaking in a fast and foreign tongue. Briefly, she wondered how Saladin was explaining the presence of a pale-faced woman in a woolly hat who was accompanying him.

With the helicopter lights flickering they flew over the night-time countryside to an airstrip, where a private jet was waiting. Aware of the veiled glances of his advisors, Livvy boarded the sleek plane, whose sides were adorned with the royal crest, startled to discover that she and the sheikh would be sitting separately during the flight.

She wondered if he saw her look of surprise just before one of the stewards ushered her through a door at the rear, to a much smaller section of the plane— though, admittedly, one that contained its own bed. Pulling out her books and music from her holdall, she looked around. Actually, there was a TV screen—and a neat little bathroom offering a tempting display of soaps and perfume. But even so…

Moments later, Saladin came to find her—all quietly

brooding power as he stood in the doorway with his cool black eyes surveying her.

'You are satisfied with your seat, I hope?' he questioned.

She was trying hard not to show she was hurt—but suddenly it wasn't easy to bite back the feelings that were bubbling up inside her. 'I wasn't expecting us to be sitting apart. Not after...' She clamped her lips shut, aware of having said too much. Did expressing vulnerability count as tenderness? she wondered.

He glanced over his shoulder before lowering his voice. 'Not after having had sex with you—is that what you mean?'

'It doesn't matter,' she mumbled.

'It does,' he said, suddenly breaking into an angry torrent of Jazratian, which was directed at the hapless steward who had appeared at the doorway behind him, but who now beat a hasty retreat. 'It matters because I'm afraid this is how things are going to be from now on.'

She stared at him, not quite understanding what he meant until his stony expression told her more clearly than any words could have done. 'You mean—?'

'What happened in England must stay in England, for we cannot be intimate in Jazratan,' he said. 'The laws of my country are very strict on such matters—and it would offend my people deeply if it was discovered that I was having sex with an unmarried woman. Particularly an unmarried foreigner.' He shrugged, as if to take some of the heat from his words. 'For I am the sheikh and you are my employee, Livvy, and from now on we will not be stepping outside the boundaries of those roles.'

It was several moments before Livvy could trust herself to speak, and if the giant plane hadn't already been taxiing down the runway, she honestly thought she might have run up to the steward and demanded they let her out.

But she couldn't. She had agreed to take the job and she was going to have to behave like a professional. And anyway—mightn't this strategy be the best strategy for keeping her emotions protected? If she and Saladin were to be segregated, it would be very difficult to foster any kind of attachment to him. So even though his words hurt, somehow she found the strength to force a careless smile onto her lips.

'Well, that's a relief,' she said.

His black eyes narrowed. 'A relief?'

'Sure. I've got a lot of reading I want to get through before we land. I told you it was a long time since I'd worked with horses.' With a wave of her hand, she gestured towards the books she'd just unpacked. 'So I'd better have a browse through these. Reacquaint myself with the species, even if it's only theoretical—until I get to meet Burkaan. So please don't let me keep you,' she added. 'I'll be perfectly happy here on my own.'

His face was a picture—as if he'd just realised that in effect she was *dismissing* him—yet he could hardly object to her demand for privacy after what he'd just said.

But once he'd gone, and she was left with the opened but unread pages of *Healing Horses Naturally*, Livvy found herself staring out of the window at the black sky as England receded, unable to deny the sudden pain that clenched like a vice around her heart.

He'd made her sound…

Like a cliché.

An unmarried foreign woman he was forbidden to have sex with.

She closed her eyes. He had come to the house determined to employ her, and for a while she had resisted him. Had he looked at her and wondered whether seduction was a price he was prepared to pay in order to guarantee her services? She bit her lip.

Even when she'd told him that she was a virgin— and a twenty-nine-year-old virgin, to boot... A lot of men might have stopped at that point. But not Saladin. Had he guessed that sex would make her eager to do his bidding? Did he realise that she would find it very difficult to refuse to work for him after what had taken place between them?

Damn him.

So stop letting him take control, she thought. *Be grateful that he's shown you are capable of sexual pleasure but also be grateful that he has put this barrier between you, because there is no future with Saladin and there never can be.*

She picked up the cup of jasmine tea that had just been put on the table by a slightly nervous-looking steward.

She was going to have to start being rational. She was here on a life-changing salary to help his horse, and she would do her utmost to accomplish that. The sex she must forget. She *had* to.

She slept for almost six hours and, when she awoke, discovered that the little shower was much better than the one at home. Afterwards she felt a million times better and was just tucking into a bowl of delicious porridge topped with iced mango when the curtain between the two sections of the plane was drawn back, and she looked up to see Saladin standing there.

It was slightly disconcerting that he'd changed from his Western clothes into an outfit more befitting a desert sheikh, because it only seemed to emphasise the vast gulf between them. Gone were the trousers, sweater and cashmere coat, and in their place were flowing robes of pure silk that completely covered him, yet hinted at the hard body beneath. His ebony hair was now hidden by a headdress, held in place by a circlet of knotted scarlet cord—and against the pale material his golden-dark features looked forbidding.

He looked like a fantasy.

Like a stranger.

And that was exactly what he was, Livvy reminded herself grimly.

His eyes fixed on her, he waited, and she was sure he expected her to scramble to her feet, but she simply finished her mouthful of porridge and gave him a faint smile.

'Morning,' she said.

He frowned before slowly inclining his head, as if forcing himself to respond civilly to her casual greeting. 'Good morning. Did you sleep well during the flight?'

'Like a dormouse, as they say in France.' Again, she smiled. 'Did you?'

Saladin felt the pounding of a pulse at his temple, her glib response only adding to his growing annoyance and frustration. No, he had not slept well, for the night had seemed endless. He had tossed and turned and eventually had drawn up one of the blinds to stare out at the jewelled and inky sky as the plane travelled through the night towards Jazratan. It had been a long time since he'd endured such restlessness. Not since...

But the realisation that he was comparing simple sexual frustration to the worst time of his life filled him with an angry guilt. Pushing aside the turmoil of his thoughts, he acknowledged the insolent way in which Livvy Miller was leaning back on her elbows, watching him. Her amber eyes were hooded and her lips gleamed from the mouthful of jasmine tea she had just drunk. How dared she continue to drink and eat in his presence?

He had told her there would be no more intimacy, but he certainly hadn't given her permission to abandon all protocol. Didn't she realise that there was an etiquette that needed to be adhered to whenever he entered the room? You did not greet the king of Jazratan with such blatant carelessness, and this was something she needed to be aware of before she arrived at the palace.

'You are supposed to stand when I enter the room,' he said coolly.

'Am I?' She fixed him with a deliberate look of challenge. 'As I recall, you seemed to prefer it when I was lying down.'

'Livvy!' He glanced behind him as he ground out his protest, feeling the instant rush of heat to his groin. 'You mustn't—'

'Mustn't what?' she interrupted in a low tone. 'Tell it like it is? Well, I'm sorry, Saladin, but I don't intend to be a hypocrite. I accept the intimacy ban you've imposed because, now I've had time to think about it, I can understand it and I think it's a good idea. But if you think I'm going to be sinking to the ground into a curtsy and lowering my eyes demurely whenever you appear, then you are very much mistaken.'

Her passionate insolence wasn't something Saladin was used to, and he was shocked into a momentary silence. He wanted to do a number of things—all of which seemed to contradict themselves. He wanted to kiss her and to simultaneously push her as far away from him as possible. He wanted never to see her again and yet he wanted to feast his eyes on her in a leisurely visual feast. Suddenly he realised that here was one person—one *woman*—who would not be moulded to his will, and with a shock it suddenly dawned on him why that was. *Because he needed her more than she needed him.*

He could not expel her for insubordination—well, he could, but his stallion would only suffer as a result. And even though he was paying way over the odds for an expertise she had warned him herself might not work, he suspected that the money didn't mean as much to her as it might to someone else.

Did it? Or had her initial reluctance to take the job simply been the work of a clever negotiator? Perhaps he should test her out.

'Surely a little civility wouldn't go amiss since I am rewarding you so handsomely for your work.'

'You're *paying* me, Saladin—not *rewarding* me,' she contradicted. 'You were the one who made the over-inflated offer in the first place, so please don't start reneging on it now. And if you want me to show you respect, I'm afraid you will have to earn it.'

'*Earn* it?' he echoed incredulously.

'Yes. Is that such an extraordinary proposition?'

He gave a short laugh. 'It is certainly one that has never been put to me before.'

She stood up then, clenching her hands into two small fists and sucking in an unsteady breath as she looked at him. 'I'm not a complete fool, Saladin,' she hissed. 'I'm fully aware that you seduced me for a purpose. And it worked.'

He looked into the amber eyes that blazed as brightly as her fiery hair. He thought how magnificent she looked when she was berating him, and suddenly he felt a lump rise in his throat. 'Believe me when I tell you this,' he said huskily. 'I seduced you because I wanted you.'

Livvy heard the sudden passion that had deepened his words and something inside her melted. Stupid how she'd almost forgotten what they'd just been arguing about. Stupid how her body was just *craving* for him to touch her.

Did he feel that, too? Was she imagining the slight move he made towards her, when suddenly the plaintive lament of what sounded like *bagpipes* broke into her thoughts and shattered the tense atmosphere. Disorientated, she met Saladin's gaze and it was as if the noise had brought him to his senses, too, because he stiffened and stepped away from her, and in his eyes flared something cold and bleak.

'What the hell is that?' she whispered.

Her question seemed to shake him out of his sombre reverie, though it took a moment before his eyes cleared and he answered. 'A hangover from my great-grandfather's holidays at your own royal family's Scottish residence,' he said. 'He was very impressed by the bagpipes that were used to wake everyone in the morning. After that he decided that they would become a permanent feature of Jazratian life. Thus a returning sheikh is always greeted on his arrival by the unmistakable sound of Scotland.'

'It's certainly very novel.'

'You will find much about my country that surprises you, Livvy,' he replied. 'In a moment I will leave the aircraft and one of the stewards will indicate when it is appropriate for you to do the same. There will be transport waiting to take you to my palace.'

She screwed up her eyes as she looked at him. 'So I won't even be travelling with you?'

He shook his head. 'No. My homecoming is always greeted with a certain amount of celebration. There will be crowds lining the route, and it would not sit well with my people were I to return to the palace in the company of a foreign female, no matter how skilled she might be in her particular field.'

'Right,' she said.

'You will be given your own very comfortable suite of rooms. Once you have settled in, I will send one of my advisors to take you to the stable complex, so that you can meet the vets and the grooms, and get to work on Burkaan straight away. You will, however, take meals with me.'

Without waiting for a response, he turned and walked away with a swish of his silken robes. And if Livvy felt momentarily frustrated by his sudden indifference, that wasn't what was currently occupying her thoughts. It was the way he had looked during those few moments when she'd thought he was going to reach out and touch her.

Because when the smoky passion had cleared from

his eyes, it had left behind a flicker of something haunting. The trace of an emotion that she wouldn't necessarily have associated with a man like Saladin.

Something that looked awfully like guilt.

CHAPTER TEN

LIVVY STOOD BENEATH the bright Jazratian sunshine and looked around her with a sense of awe and a slight sense of feeling displaced—as if she couldn't quite believe she was here in Saladin's homeland, and that it was Christmas Eve.

The Al Mektala stable complex was lavish, and no expense had been spared in providing for the needs and comfort of over a hundred horses. She'd read about places like this, in those long-ago days when an equestrian magazine had never been far from her hand—but had never imagined herself actually working in one.

Fine sand paddocks were edged with lines of palm trees, which provided welcome shade, but plenty of areas had been laid to grass and it was curiously restful—if a little bizarre—to see large patches of green set against the harsh backdrop of the desert landscape. There were plush air-conditioned boxes for the horses and even a dappled and cool pool in which they could swim. Grooms, physiotherapists and jockeys—all clad in the distinctive Al Mektala livery of indigo and silver—swarmed around the place as efficiently as ants working in harmony together.

After arriving at the palace Livvy had been shown

to a large suite of rooms, where she'd changed into jodhpurs and a shirt and then followed the servant who had been dispatched to take her to the stables. She hadn't been expecting to find Saladin waiting for her—and she certainly wasn't expecting to see him similarly attired in riding clothes, his fingers curving rather distractingly around a riding whip.

She had to force her thoughts away from how lusciously the jodhpurs were clinging to his narrow hips and hugging the powerful shafts of his long legs. It was difficult not to let her gaze linger on the way his billowing silk shirt gave definition to the rock-like torso beneath, making him resemble the kind of buccaneering hero you might find on some Sunday-night TV drama. She told herself that she wasn't going to remember the way he had held her when he'd been making love to her, or the way it had felt to have him deep inside her. She wasn't going to think about how good it had felt to be kissed by him—or the way she'd cried out as she had reached her climax, over and over again. She was here to see if she could help his horse—and that was the *only* reason she was here.

But it was hard to stand so close to him and to resist the desire to reach out and touch him, even though she was doing her best to keep her smile cool and professional.

'So what do you think of my stables, Livvy?'

She smiled. 'As you predicted—it's very interesting to see what you've done in such an extreme climate. And it's all very impressive—just as I would have expected,' she observed as she glanced around. 'Perhaps I could see Burkaan now?'

Once again Saladin felt that inexplicable conflict

within him. He was irritated by her lack of desire to make small talk with him—yet couldn't help but admire her cool professionalism. Just as he was irritated with himself for having almost reached out to her on the plane, when temptation had wrapped itself around his skin like a silken snare. But he had stopped himself just in time, and that was a good thing, although it hadn't felt particularly easy at the time. Because he'd forced himself to remember that he was back in Jazratan where expectations were different and where the memory of Alya was at its strongest. Here, his role was rigidly defined, and casual sex with foreigners simply was not on the agenda. He needed to put that delicious interlude out of his mind and to see whether or not she could live up to her reputation.

Raising his hand, he indicated to the waiting groom that his horse should be brought outside, and he felt his heart quicken in anticipation, as if hoping that some miracle had happened while he'd been away and that Burkaan would come trotting out into the yard with his former vitality.

But the reality shocked and saddened him. The sight of his beloved stallion being led from his stable, looking like a shadow of his former self, made Saladin's heart clench painfully in his chest. The magnificent racehorse's frame seemed even more diminished, and his normally glossy black coat looked lacklustre and dull. The stallion was usually happy, but he was not happy now. Saladin could almost read the anguish and the pain in his eyes as he bared his teeth at his master.

'Don't go near him yet,' he warned Livvy. 'He's been very vicious. Few people can get close to him. Even me.'

But to his annoyance and a concern he couldn't quite hide, she completely ignored his words, moving so quietly towards the horse that she could have been a ghost as she held out her hand in a gesture of peace.

'It's okay,' she said to the animal, in the softest, most musical voice he had ever heard. 'I'm not going to hurt you. It's okay, Burkaan. It's going to be fine.'

Burkaan was more used to being spoken to in Jazratian, and even before his accident had been known for his intolerance of strangers, but Saladin watched in amazement as Livvy moved closer to the powerful animal. There was a split second when he expected the horse to lash out at her and braced himself in readiness to snatch the stubborn woman out of harm's way. But the moment did not come. Instead, she slowly reached out and began to stroke his neck. And Burkaan let her!

'It's all right,' she was crooning quietly. 'I've come to help you. Do you know that, Burkaan? Do you?'

The horse gave a little whinny, and Saladin felt his throat constrict with something that felt uncomfortably like hope. But he knew better than anyone that misplaced hope was the most painful emotion of all, and he drove it from his heart with a ruthlessness he'd learned a long time ago. Just because the horse was prepared to allow the Englishwoman to approach and to touch him didn't mean a thing.

'I wonder, could you ask the groom to walk him around the yard a little?' she said. 'Just so I can see how badly he's injured?'

Saladin nodded and spoke to the groom, and the stricken stallion was led forward and began to hobble around the yard.

'You will note that he has injured his—'

'His near foreleg,' Livvy interrupted crisply, her gaze following the horse as it slowly made its way to the other side of the yard. 'Yes, I can see that. He's clearly in a lot of pain and he's hopping to try to compensate. Okay. I've seen everything I need to see. Please ask the groom to bring him back now, and put him in his box.'

Feeling like her tame linguist, Saladin relayed her instructions to the groom, and once Burkaan had been led back into his box, Livvy turned to face him. He thought her smile looked forced, and he wondered if she was aware that the bright Jazratian sunshine was making her hair look like liquid fire. And, oh, how he would love to feel the burn of it against his fingers again.

'I'm just going to try a few things out,' she said. 'So I'd prefer it if you and everyone else would leave now.'

Disbelief warred with a grudging admiration as she spoke to him, because Saladin realised that once again she was *dismissing* him. She really *was* fond of taking control, wasn't she? He had never been dominated by a woman before, and he was finding it more exciting than he could ever have anticipated—but he would not tolerate it. No way. Surely she must realise that this was *his* stable and *his* horse, and of course he would wish to observe her. He fixed her with a steady look. 'I'm not going anywhere, Livvy,' he said. 'I want to be here.'

She sucked in a deep breath. 'I'm sorry, but I prefer to work alone.'

'I don't care. I want to be here,' he repeated.

She narrowed her eyes as if trying to weigh up whether there was any point in further argument, before obviously coming to the most sensible conclusion.

'Very well,' she said. 'But I don't want any distractions. You must keep very quiet and not interfere. I want you to stand over there out of the way, to keep very still and not say a word. Do you understand?'

Saladin's mouth thinned into a grim smile as her cool words washed over him. One thing he *did* understand was that nobody else had ever spoken to him like this before, not even Alya—especially not Alya, who had been the most agreeable woman ever made.

Instinct made him want to march over to Livvy and pull rank and ask her who the hell she thought she was talking to. To remind her that he was the sheikh and he would damned well do as he pleased. Yet what alternative did he have but to accede to her demands, when the welfare of his beloved horse was of far greater importance than his own sense of pride and position?

'Yes, Livvy,' he said drily. 'I think I get the general idea.'

Afterwards he would try to work out exactly what she had done to Burkaan, but, apart from a vague impression of her laying her palms on the animal's injured foreleg, her time with the horse seemed to pass in a blur. Maybe it was because for once Saladin got the distinct impression that her words had been true. She really didn't want him there, and would have preferred it if he had gone back to the palace as she'd requested. It was certainly the first time in his life that he had been completely ignored.

Because sheikhs were never ignored and people were always conscious of his presence. No matter how large an official function or social gathering, everyone always knew exactly where he was situated, although they often pretended not to. Nobody ever left a room while he remained in it, and nobody ever turned their back on him.

But none of this seemed relevant as he watched Livvy whispering into Burkaan's ear and running feather-light fingertips over the horse's injured limb and then stroking their way over his back. To his surprise, the stallion seemed to tolerate almost every touch she made—only jerking back his head and showing his teeth on two occasions. Eventually, she straightened up and wiped the palms of her hands down over her jodhpurs, and he could see sweat beading her pale brow.

'I've finished now,' she said. 'I'll see him later. Make sure he gets some rest and is undisturbed until I do.'

He saw her glance at her watch and realised that he had effectively backed himself into a corner. He had told her—quite correctly—that they would be occupying separate sections of the palace. He had told her that their lives would cross only at mealtimes and when she was hands-on with Burkaan. Yet now the thought of that did not please him—on the contrary, it positively *rankled*. He had found it necessary to lay out his boundaries during the flight over, in order to emphasise to her that the sex had meant nothing—and he had been expecting a host of objections from her, or maybe even a petulant sulk. Because women always tried to cling on to him when he rejected them—as reject them he inevitably did.

But Livvy was showing no signs of clinging—or sulking. She had travelled separately to the palace without protest, and, on arriving at her suite of rooms, had apparently made some complimentary comment to one of the servants about the ancient tiled floors and the beauty of the palace gardens. And ironically, he had found himself curiously unsettled by her apparent acceptance of the situation in which she now found herself.

'We have plenty of time before lunch,' he said. 'Perhaps you would care to ride with me?'

For a moment, Livvy felt temptation wash over her as his suggestion brought back echoes of a life she had left far behind. She thought of being in the saddle again and the feeling of having all that impressive horse power beneath her. She thought of the warm, desert breeze against her skin and the incomparable sense of freedom that riding always gave her, but, resolutely, she shook her head. 'I don't ride anymore.'

'Why not?'

She met the question in his narrowed eyes. 'Because riding demands time and commitment and money—and I've been too busy running my business to have any of those things.'

'But you have time now,' he pointed out coolly. 'And money isn't a consideration.'

'It's out of the question,' she said. 'I'm completely out of practice.'

There was a pause. 'And maybe you're scared of getting back on a horse after so long away?'

His unexpected insight caught her off guard. Was that why she answered him so truthfully?

'Maybe a little,' she agreed. But it wasn't fear of the horse that frightened her. It was the thought of re-entering a world that had brought her pain and that now seemed so long ago it might have happened to another person.

'Then, why not get back in the saddle?' His voice

deepened. 'Kill your fear by confronting it. Don't they say that the more you practise, the better you get?'

And suddenly there was an undeniable sexual innuendo whispering in the air around them and whipping up an unspoken need inside her. She could feel sudden tension heating her skin, and the tips of her breasts had grown suddenly sensitive. She could feel it in the way her lips parted, as if silently inviting him to kiss them—and, oh, how she wanted him to kiss her.

Livvy stared at Saladin as she tried to dampen down the rising tide of desire. To remind herself of the way he'd treated her since she had agreed to treat his horse. He had kept her away from him during the flight and ordered separate journeys to the palace, where she had been allocated quarters in the staff section. She didn't have a problem with that—because she *was* staff. What she *did* have a problem with was his assumption that he could treat her like some kind of plaything. Act icy one minute and then flirt with her the next. Well, he had better learn that it didn't work like that. She didn't dare let it.

'I don't want it to come back,' she said.

'Why not?'

She glanced down at the tips of her riding boots, which were covered in fine dust, before lifting her gaze to meet the jet-dark gleam of his eyes. 'Because when I split with Rupert I walked away from riding. I bolted—and I shut the stable door behind me. I left my job, realising that I had no appetite to face the knowing looks and the knowledge that he'd been sleeping with my best friend.'

'You could have found different stables.'

'I could. But horse riding is a very small world,

and gossip always follows you around. I wanted to be known as more than the woman who'd been involved in a spicy scandal. I wanted a clean break and that's what I got. The old Livvy has gone and so has the world she lived in. I'm not looking to recapture something from the past—I'm here because I'm trying to take care of my future. So if you've finished with the interrogation, I'd like someone to show me back to my room because this palace is so big, I don't trust myself not to get lost.'

With a thoughtful look, he inclined his head. 'Certainly. I will show you to your suite myself.'

'There's really no need. A servant will do.'

'My servants don't speak English.'

'I'm quite happy to forego conversation.'

'I will show you to your room, Livvy,' he said, with silky insistence. 'And please don't oppose me just for the sake of it, or you will discover how quickly my tolerance limit can be reached.'

His reprimand was stern and maybe it was justified, but as Livvy fell into step beside him she realised that even *opposing* him was making her feel things she didn't want to feel. Desire was throbbing through her body and making her want to squirm with frustration. It was all she could do not to reach out and touch him—to whisper her fingers possessively over his riding shirt and feel the hard torso beneath. Was it because he'd been her only lover that she was feeling this way? Was she building it up in her head because he'd taken her virginity so that what had happened seemed powerful and significant?

Yet maybe that wasn't so surprising when sex with Saladin had seemed so *easy*. It had happened so naturally. It had felt as if she'd been waiting all her life for the desert sheikh to make love to her. As if she hadn't been complete until he had completed her.

And wasn't that the way it was supposed to feel?

Blocking out the disturbing thoughts that were threatening to overwhelm her, she focused her attention on the splendour of her surroundings instead. The temperature dropped as they passed through the shaded portico into the main palace, where the polished floors were deliciously cool and smooth.

They crossed a courtyard and, on the far side, Livvy saw a shining silver bower, festooned with tumbling roses of scarlet and orange and pink. Glittering brightly in the midday sun, it was topped with an intricate silver structure of filigree metal flowers and leaves and Livvy's footsteps came to a halt. 'Wow,' she said slowly. 'What is that place?'

By her side Saladin stiffened as he followed the direction of her eyes. 'That is the Faddi gate, leading to the palace rose garden,' he said abruptly.

'Oh, it's beautiful. Could we go that way?'

But suddenly he seemed to be having difficulty controlling his emotions and Livvy looked up to see a tiny nerve working frantically at his temple and that his mouth had hardened with an expression she couldn't quite fathom. He shook his head.

'The gardeners are working there,' he said abruptly. 'And they do not like to be observed. Come, I will take you a different way.'

He remained tense for a minute or two, but as they walked towards her rooms he began to recount some of the history of Jazratan and of the palace itself. And somehow the change of subject was enough to make him relax—and Livvy relaxed, too, so that after a while she found herself engrossed in the things he was telling her. He talked about battles that had been fought and won by his ancestors, of sheikhs whose lifeblood had seeped like rust onto the desert sands. He told her about the brave mount who had led one particular victorious battle—a forerunner to his own, beloved Burkaan.

She realised then why his horse was so important to him, and it had nothing to do with money, or even a close bond that transcended his royal status. Because Burkaan was a link between the past and the future. If the stallion was put out to stud, then his illustrious line would continue. And continuity was the lifeblood of a ruling monarch.

He's so different from you, Livvy thought. *So don't ever make the mistake of thinking it could be any other way than this.*

They had just reached her door when Saladin suddenly reached out to wrap his fingers around her wrist, and the unexpected gesture shocked Livvy into stillness. She wondered if he could feel the sudden hammering of her pulse. He must do. It sounded so thunderous to her own ears she was surprised it hadn't brought the servants running.

'Thank you for what you did today,' he said.

'I did very little.'

'On the contrary. You calmed a horse who has been nothing but vicious since his accident. It was the first time I've seen a fleeting moment of peace in his eyes.'

And Livvy found herself looking into *his* eyes, helplessly snared by their ebony light. She'd seen many emotions in them since that snowy afternoon when he had first walked into her life. She'd seen them harden with irritation and determination. She'd seen them soften with desire and lust. And she'd seen them cloud over with something that had looked very like sorrow as they had stared at the Faddi gate leading to the rose garden. Did Saladin have his own dark demons raging within him? she wondered.

Reluctantly, she pulled her hand away from his—even though deep down she wanted to curl her fingers into his palm, like a cat settling down for the evening. But that way lay danger. He'd already set out the boundaries and, even though her body wanted to push at those boundaries, she recognised that distance from Saladin made perfect sense.

'You really must excuse me,' she said, bringing a note of formality into her voice. 'I need to call England to check that Peppa is okay and that the snow hasn't caused any lasting damage.' She smiled. 'I'll see you at lunch—presumably you will send someone to collect me?'

And with that, she walked into her suite, quietly closing the door—not caring that he was still standing there looking darkly displeased by her dismissal. Not caring about anything other than a need to put some distance between them before she did something crazy like fling herself against that hard and virile body and beg him to make love to her again.

CHAPTER ELEVEN

IT WASN'T AS easy as he had thought it would be.

It wasn't easy at all.

With an impatient flick of his hand, Saladin waved the servant away and lowered his body into the deep tub of steaming water. How was it possible to feel exhausted when you had only just risen from your bed? Could it have anything to do with the fact that he'd spent yet another sleepless night frustratedly recalling that erotic fireside encounter when the innocent Livvy Miller had cried out her passion in his arms?

Maybe he'd been naive to think it would be easy to adhere to his self-imposed sex ban when she was living here at the palace. When thoughts of her kept drifting into his mind at the most inconvenient times—usually without warning or provocation. Sometimes he found himself sitting through meetings of state and thinking about her pale skin and fiery hair. About the way he had cupped her narrow hips and driven into that slender body. He would sit uncomfortably with a massive erection hidden by his flowing robes, and wonder why he had insisted that she remain totally off limits.

Because he could not trash his sacred memories of

the past by indulging in a casual fling, especially here in the palace.

For a while he lay in the cooling water and thought about the long days that had passed since Livvy's arrival. The Englishwoman had settled in well—better than he could ever have anticipated. She had worked diligently with Burkaan four times a day and, although she grudgingly permitted his presence at these sessions, she had made it clear that she expected total silence from him—and he had found himself complying!

At other times he had barely seen her. She hadn't seemed to mind missing any of the holiday celebrations she would have enjoyed back in England. He'd heard from the servants that she spent much of her time reading on the shaded terraces outside her suite. And it infuriated him to realise that it would be completely inappropriate to disturb her there, even though he was master of all he surveyed. He felt as if he was caught in a trap of his own making. Sometimes he caught a glimpse of her as she made her way out to the sprawling expanse of the palace gardens and watched as she peered through the Faddi gate. And wondered why it was no longer Alya's face he could see in his mind, but the face of the freckly Englishwoman.

Because she was off limits?

Because she wasn't coming on to him? That was something else he found it hard to get his head round. There had been no coy glances or lingering looks. She hadn't been flaunting her body in close-fitting clothes to torment him with memories of what lay beneath. No, she had acted with an admirable—if infuriating—decorum.

Only at mealtimes were the wretched rules relaxed—

and then he found himself eager to talk to her. He quizzed her about his horse's progress and gradually, once she had lost some of the new guarded expression she seemed to assume around him, she began to open up a little more. It was a unique situation, he realised, for rarely did he have the opportunity—or inclination—to get to know a woman. Women were there for his sexual pleasure, and once he had taken his fill he walked away. But with Livvy, there was no opportunity for sexual pleasure. And not only was he unable to walk away—bizarrely he found he didn't want to. This pale and stubborn Englishwoman was intriguing him more than he had expected to be intrigued.

She told him about getting on her first horse at the age of three, and her mother's love of riding. Of her own increasing skill on horseback and the way the two of them used to gallop across the dewy fields around Wightwick Manor. She spoke of frosty landscapes washed pink with the light from the rising sun. She told him about the first time she realised that she could understand horses in a way that most people couldn't and the 'awesome feeling of responsibility' it had given her. She described the day she'd brought home her first rosette, aged six, and then her first shiny silver trophy a year later.

It was after one such recollection after lunch one day that he heard her voice falter and Saladin found himself leaning back in his chair to study her.

'You must miss it,' he said. 'Riding.'

She gave a little shrug. 'Sometimes.'

'So what can I do to tempt you back into the saddle?'

'You can stop trying—I'm not interested.'

'Aren't you?'

She put down her golden goblet with a thud. 'No.'

And suddenly Saladin wanted to break all his own rules. He wanted to forget that he was a king and a widower and to behave like any other man. To seek pleasure and comfort when it was available. To try to rid himself of some of this obsession he had for the titian-haired Englishwoman. Because soon there would be no reason for her to remain. Burkaan was improving daily—everyone had commented on the fact. Soon she would be headed back to England and he would never see her again. Because deep down he suspected that, unlike other lovers, Livvy would not be interested in a brief relationship back in England, simply to burn their passion away. He suspected that she would disapprove of such a cold-blooded suggestion.

So couldn't it burn itself out here and now? Wasn't he the king of all he surveyed, who could change the unspoken rules of his land, just as long as he wasn't blatant about it?

'Ride with me today, Livvy,' he said suddenly. 'For mercy's sake—what harm can it do?'

Livvy looked at him, acknowledging the suddenly urgent note in his voice. She wanted to refuse. To tell him that it felt too poignant, too intimate, too…too *everything*. And yet…yet…

She looked into the gleam of his black eyes. The temptation was strong and her thoughts made it even stronger. What harm could one little ride do, on one of the sheikh's magnificent horses, as she had been longing to do for weeks? To be alone with the desert king—far away from the watchful eyes of the palace servants. 'I'll ride with you later,' she said. 'After Burkaan's final session of the day.'

The state of excitement inside her for the next few hours was disproportionate to the short ride that he'd undoubtedly scheduled. At least, that was what Livvy told herself. But no matter how much she tried to minimise the impact of some time alone with Saladin away from the palace, nothing could get rid of the fizz of excitement in her blood.

Her heart was pounding as she swung herself up into the saddle with Saladin watching her closely, his hand on the reins.

'Okay?' he questioned.

She nodded as she felt the first ripple of the animal's power beneath her. 'Okay,' she echoed softly.

The beautiful chestnut mare he'd given her was placid, and, with Saladin mounting a much bigger roan stallion, they trotted out of the stable complex side by side onto the hard desert sands. The rhythmic pounding of the horses' hooves was both soothing and exhilarating as they began to canter. The sun was low and the sky was an inverted bowl of deepest blue as Livvy breathed in the warm air. She felt...*alive*. The most alive she'd felt since...

Since Saladin had made love to her.

She turned to look at him, thinking that he resembled a figure from a fantasy tale. No jodhpurs today—instead, his white headdress billowed behind him and his silken robes clung to the hard contours of his body as he rode alongside her.

'How do you know your way around?' she questioned. 'Aren't you afraid of getting lost?'

He gave a brief smile. 'I grew up in this land,' he said. 'And it is as familiar to me as my own skin.'

'Really?' She thought using his skin as a comparison

probably wasn't the best idea, under the circumstances—but she kept her expression neutral. 'In what way?'

He shrugged as he slowed his horse down. 'You see nothing but sand, but I see ridges and undulations on the surface where the winds have blown—and I can read the wind by sight and sound as others can read music. I know where there are underground rivers and lakes, where vegetation can thrive and provide shelter. And I always make sure I'm carrying adequate supplies of water and a compass—as well as a cell phone.' He flicked her another brief smile. 'Would you like me to take you to an oasis?'

She thought at first that he must be joking, because it sounded so *corny*. She half remembered some pop song her mother used to love. Something about midnight at an oasis. Livvy gripped the reins a little tighter as she met the gleaming question in his black eyes and suddenly she wondered what the hell was making her hesitate. When else in her life was she ever going to get the opportunity to see an oasis?

'I'd love to,' she said.

'Then, come,' he urged, and when he saw the look of hesitation on her face he gave a quick smile. *'Come.'* Pressing his knees into his horse's flanks, he set off at a gallop and after a moment's hesitation Livvy started after him.

It came back within seconds—that raw exhilaration and sheer *joy*. She'd forgotten the speed and sense of power you got when you were riding a horse at full pelt, and any lingering reservations were melted away as she galloped after the sheikh.

Over hard and undulating sands they rode—with nothing but the heavy sound of hooves pounding. They rode until Saladin slowed down the pace so that they could mount a steep incline, and Livvy's breath died in her throat when she saw what was on the other side. For there was an unexpectedly wide gleam of water surrounded by grasses and a line of lush palm trees that provided acres of shade.

'Oh, wow,' she said softly. 'A real oasis.'

'Did you think it was a mirage?' he questioned drily.

The truthful answer would have been yes, because nothing felt quite real as Livvy's horse followed Saladin's down to the desert lake, and she jumped down to lead her mount towards the water. She could hear the strange squawking of a bird in one of the palm trees and the glugging splash as the two thirsty animals drank. Saladin gestured for her to tether her horse in the shade next to his, while he drew out a canister of water and offered it to her.

Rarely had any drink ever tasted as delicious as this, and Livvy gulped it down with gratitude and a strange sense of being at peace with herself. She was standing beneath the shade of a palm tree and Saladin was taking the container from her suddenly boneless fingers and drinking from it himself. And she wondered how sharing water with a man could seem so ridiculously *intimate*. Because they had shared so much more than this? She watched the swallowing movement of his neck and suddenly her mouth felt dry again—even though she'd just drunk about half a litre.

He didn't say a word as he put the empty container back and then took her by the hand, leading her towards the cool canopy provided by the palm trees—and she didn't ask him where he was taking her or what he was about to do when he got there, because she knew.

It was obvious from the sudden tension in the fingers that were firmly laced around her own. The way in which her heart had suddenly started to race in response. He came to a halt when their faces were shadowed by the cool fronds above their heads, and her face was grave as he removed the wide-brimmed hat from her head and placed it on the ground.

'Saladin,' she said breathlessly as he framed her face in the palms of his hands.

His voice was quiet, but insistent. 'I'm going to kiss you.'

'But you said—'

'I said that we couldn't have sex in the palace, but we aren't in the palace now. Are we?'

She shook her head, wishing he'd made it sound a little less *anatomical*, wishing he'd responded with a few romantic words in what was a very romantic setting. But maybe she would have to make do with this—along with the realisation that at least he wasn't making mirages of his own. He wasn't wooing her with empty promises—he was telling it the way it was. And anyway by then he was kissing her and all her objections were forgotten as she opened her lips beneath his, because hadn't she been missing this, more than she would have ever thought possible?

His hands were hot and urgent as they raked through her hair and over her body, and her own were equally hungry as they explored the hardness of his magnificent physique. Impatiently, he slithered off her jodhpurs and shirt before peeling off his own silken robes, and Livvy gasped to discover that he was completely naked beneath.

'It is another characteristic we share with the Scots,'

he murmured as he spread the robes onto the sand to make a silky bed for them. 'Who I believe wear nothing beneath their kilts?'

But Livvy didn't answer because by then she felt as if she were in the middle of a dream—the most amazing dream of her life—as he laid her down. His eyes were unreadable as he moved over her and made his first thrust, and she gasped out his name as he entered her.

'It's good?'

She bit her lip and moaned. 'It's terrible.'

He laughed, but then his voice changed to a note she'd never heard before as he began to move inside her. 'Oh, Livvy.'

She didn't answer. There were things she'd like to have known and questions that maybe she should have asked. But she didn't. She couldn't. She was powerless to do anything other than respond to the feel of Saladin deep inside her. Because by then she had started to come, and there wasn't a thing she could do to stop it.

They rode back after night had fallen, even though Livvy had initially been fearful of crossing the dark desert on horseback. But Saladin had run the tip of his tongue along the edge of her lips, and she had felt him smile as he answered her question.

'I told you that I know this desert as well as my own body,' he said softly. 'Don't you realise that there's a great big celestial map overhead?'

That had been the point when she'd looked up at the stars that she'd been too distracted to notice before. The brightest stars she'd ever seen—silver bright against the indigo backdrop of the sky. And there was the moon rising in splendour—a bright, gleaming curve above the palm trees where they'd spent the past two hours making love. Livvy felt a lump rise in her throat. It was like a fairy tale, she thought.

Except that it wasn't a fairy tale. It was nothing but a brief interlude, and Saladin had already warned her that real life would soon intrude.

He had pulled her against him after they'd dressed and brushed away stray grains of sand from their clothing. He had tilted up her chin so that she was caught in the dark gleam of his eyes and, in that moment, she'd felt very close to falling in love with him.

But his black eyes had been empty. The barrier was back, she realised, with a sinking heart.

'You know that when we return—'

'I'm to act as though nothing's happened.'

His eyes glittered in the starlight. 'How did you know that's what I was going to say?'

'Wasn't it?'

He seemed surprised by her calm response. Was that why he provided an explanation she hadn't asked for?

'This cannot happen within the walls of the palace,' he said. 'It would place you at a disadvantage were people to find out that we were having some sort of relationship.'

'Sweet of you to be concerned about my reputation, Saladin. Are you sure it isn't your own you're worried about?'

'I don't think you understand,' he said, his voice growing cool. 'It will impede your work if there is any suggestion that we are intimate. I will not have any negative fallout because we've just had sex.'

'Because soon I'll be gone and it will all be forgotten?' she questioned lightly.

There was a pause.

'Precisely,' he said.

His honesty should have pleased her, but right then Livvy could have done without it. She wanted him to tell her soft things. Tender things. She wanted the man who had made love to her so beautifully, not this cold-eyed stranger who had taken his place and was swinging his powerful body up onto his horse. But it was a timely wake-up call, she reminded herself. Just because something *felt* like magic—didn't mean it was. She mustn't ask the impossible of a man who had not promised her anything he was incapable of delivering. She must approach this…*affair* like any other woman of her age—with enjoyment and enthusiasm and a lack of expectation. She mustn't start to care for him more than was wise, but take what was on offer and not look beyond that.

She could choose to stay or to run away—and it seemed that she had chosen to stay.

The palace gleamed like a citadel in the distance as they rode in silence towards it. They brought the horses in and handed them over to two grooms, before entering the marbled splendour of Saladin's home. A servant appeared and the sheikh spoke to him in rapid Jazratian, before walking her to the door of her suite.

The corridor was empty, and she could feel the whisper of the warm, scented air that drifted in from the nearby courtyard.

'Sleep well,' he said, and with the briefest of smiles he was gone, leaving her staring at the swish of his silken robes and wondering if she'd dreamed the whole thing.

Livvy went into her suite and slipped into a robe, once she'd showered the desert dust from her body. Afterwards, a female servant knocked on the door with a tray containing iced pomegranate juice, along with a plate of sweet cake and juicy segments of peeled fruit—but although Livvy drank, she had little appetite.

She went to stare out at the night sky, thinking about what lay ahead—knowing that the X-ray that Burkaan had undergone yesterday had shown the 'miracle' to have happened. The stallion was responding to the gift she was terrified she'd lost, and soon her skills would be redundant. No longer would she have those proud and hawklike features to gaze on during mealtimes. There would be no more passionate interludes like the one she had experienced in the desert today. She would become the ordinary person she'd been before the sheikh had awoken her. And he had awoken her in so many ways—she must never forget that. He had introduced her to sex and helped her overcome her reservations about getting on a horse. He had injected colour into a world that seemed to have become monochrome. He'd made her feel vital—and desirable. He'd made her feel that she *mattered*.

And the thought of never seeing him again was like having a knife rammed straight into the centre of her heart.

As she got into bed she found herself wondering why he hadn't married—why some beautiful royal bride hadn't been found for such an eligible man, despite his occasionally irascible nature. Perhaps he was contented with his single status. Perhaps the demands of running a country were enough to satisfy him, or he might just be one of those men who didn't want marriage. She knew he'd had countless liaisons with gorgeous models and actresses, but even so it was confusing. Surely such an autocratic man longed for an heir to carry on his blood-line? She found herself wondering why he had become so emotional the first time she'd seen the Faddi gate, but she hadn't dared bring up the subject again, and none of the servants spoke enough English for her to ask.

She got into bed and the excitement of the day must have caught up on her because very quickly she fell asleep. She thought she must be dreaming when she felt the bed dip and a rough, muscular thigh slide over hers. Heart pounding, she turned over and reached out to find a naked Saladin in bed beside her, his hard body washed silver by the moonlight flooding in from the unshuttered windows.

Her lips swollen with sleep, she stumbled out the words—half-afraid that speaking would break the spell and make him disappear. She wanted him so badly, and yet wasn't there a part of herself that despised her eagerness to have him touch her again? 'Saladin,' she whispered.

'The very same.'

'What are you doing here?'

'No ideas?' he mocked as he reached out to curve his hand over her breast. 'Such a shocking lack of imagi-nation, Livvy.'

And he bent his head to kiss her.

She started to speak but he shook his head.

'Don't say a word,' he warned softly. 'I feel that you and I have done enough talking to last a lifetime.'

'A lifetime? Well, that isn't something that is ever going to be relevant in our case, is it?'

Saladin heard the unmistakable sadness behind her defiance and wondered if she was hoping for reassurance. Perhaps thinking that because he was about to start making love to her in the palace, there was now the potential for longevity. His mouth hardened. But there wasn't, and hypocrisy and raising false hope would be an insult to a woman like Livvy. He wouldn't whisper sweet words that meant nothing, or tantalise her with glimpses of a future that could never be theirs. Nor would he torture himself with the certainty that this was *wrong*, and that he was tarnishing the memory of all that was honest and true.

Ruthlessly he blocked the voice of duty, which had been a constant sound in his head since he'd been old enough to comprehend its meaning. And concentrated on touching Livvy instead, wondering how her petite body could make him almost incoherent with lust.

The ragged moan he gave as he eased himself inside her sounded unfamiliar. Just as the feeling in his heart was unfamiliar—the sense of growing and explosive joy. He said something fervent in his native tongue and her eyes flew open in question.

'What was that you said?'

'I said that you feel as tight as one of the drums played by the Karsuruum tribe.'

Her pupils dilated still farther as she bit back a smile. 'And is that…?' There was a sudden intake of breath as he thrust deeper inside her. 'Is that supposed to be a compliment?'

'Yes,' he ground out. 'It is.'

He wanted to come immediately but he forced himself to wait. He teased her to a fever pitch—until she was whispering his name in something that sounded like a plea. And still he held back—until he felt her convulsing around him, her soft cries muffled by the pressure of his kiss as he cried out his own ragged pleasure.

Even afterwards, he didn't want to let her go. He didn't move from his position inside her, his palms possessively cupping her buttocks to maintain that sweet contact. He could feel her breath warm against his neck and the pinpoint thrust of her nipples and he thought he could have stayed like that all night.

Eventually she spoke, her voice muffled against his neck.

'I thought we weren't going to do this.'

'This?'

'Making love in the palace. That's what you said.'

'Did I?'

'You know you did.'

'Maybe when I had the chance to think about it, it seemed a little short-sighted.' He stroked her hair. 'It suddenly occurred to me that I have much experience while you have barely any at all. It seemed to make sense that while you are here you should learn from me. We are harming no one provided that we keep our liaison discreet—and I am very good at being discreet, *habibi*.'

She lifted her head and her amber eyes were suddenly serious. 'You mean, I'm to be your pupil? Like a novice rider who comes to the stables and needs to be taught everything about horses?'

'In a way, yes. But you are more to me than that.'

'I am?'

'Indeed you are. You are also a temptation I find myself unable to resist.' He saw the hope that died in her eyes as he took her hand and moved it down between his legs. 'See how you arouse me so instantly, Livvy?'

She looked down. *'Oh,'* she said, but her voice trembled a little.

'Yes, *oh.* Now stroke me,' he instructed softly. 'Whisper the tips of your fingers up and down my length. Like that. Yes. Only lighter. Oh, yes. Just like that.'

He came suddenly, his seed spilling over her fingers, and then he stroked her moist flesh until she was writhing beneath him and he had to muffle the cries of her orgasm with the pressure of his kiss.

And only when her eyelids had grown heavy and her breathing had slowed into the steady rhythm of sleep did Saladin slide from her bed and, after pulling on his robes, slip silently from the room.

CHAPTER TWELVE

BE CAREFUL WHAT you wish for.

Livvy stared up at the ceiling, aware of the minutes that were ticking away, knowing that soon Saladin would rise from her bed and leave her room—like a ghost who had never been there.

She'd told herself that she would be contented with what she had. That making love with Saladin was sublime—and she should make the most of the sexual pleasure they enjoyed, night after night.

But it was not enough—and she didn't know why.

During the day he treated her with a polite neutrality. He ate his meals with her and chatted to her, and came to the stables to watch her working with Burkaan whenever he had space in his schedule. It was hard to believe that this very *formal* sheikh was the same man whose touch always brought her to life in bed, leaving her sighing with pleasure as she snuggled up to him. But once the pleasure had worn off she was increasingly aware that he always kept something back. That there was a darkness at his core that he wouldn't share, something hidden from her and the rest of the world.

It left her feeling incomplete. As if she was getting only half the man. She knew that what they had couldn't last—but she couldn't bear to leave Jazratan without having known her lover as completely as possible. Surely that wasn't too much to ask.

So why act like his tame puppet who just accepted whatever he was prepared to dole out? Surely sexual relationships allowed for all kinds of discovery, other than the purely physical?

She rolled over on the bed and ran her fingertips along the rough rasp of his jawline.

'Saladin?'

There was a pause. 'Mmm?'

'Can I ask you something?'

Beneath the rumpled sheet, Saladin stretched his legs, and as he did so his thigh brushed against the softness of hers. She really did have the most beautiful thighs, he thought as he yawned.

As usual, he had come to her bed once darkness had fallen, driven by a fierce sexual hunger that showed no sign of abating. He knew it was a risk to his reputation—and hers—to persist in his nightly seduction, but it was a risk he was prepared to take. Because he was beginning to realise that the qualities that made her such a consummate horse whisperer were the same qualities that made her such a superb lover. She was intuitive and curious—gentle yet strong. He'd thought that the innocence that had stayed with her until a relatively late stage might have made her cautious, or wary. But he had been wrong. There had been no variation on the act of love that Olivia Miller hadn't embraced with an enthusiasm and sensuality that easily matched his own.

He tried not to react as her fingertips made dancing little movements across his chest, but he could feel the renewed throb of desire at his groin. 'You can ask me anything you wish, *habibi*—although whether or not I choose to answer it is quite another matter.'

Seemingly undeterred, a single fingertip now made a journey upwards to drift along his chin—its progress slow as it scraped against the new growth there.

'Why have you never married?'

The question came out of the blue and hit him like a slap to the face. He stilled and moved away from her. Had he been too quick to commend her? Too eager to think the best of her—his perfect lover—when deep down all she wanted to do was to probe into matters that did not concern her?

'It never ceases to amaze me,' he breathed, 'how you can be in bed with a woman and all she wants to do is talk about other women.'

He felt her stiffen beside him.

'Are you trying to change the subject?'

'What do you think?'

She clicked on a small lamp and stared at him. 'I think you are.'

'Well, then. Take the hint. Don't ask.'

'You're not the only one who doesn't *do* hints.' She tucked a strand of hair behind her ear and kept her gaze fixed steadily on him. 'I'm not asking you because I'm angling for some kind of permanent role in your life. I know what my limitations are. I know this is just sex—'

'*Just* sex?' he echoed, the taunt too much to resist as he reached for her breast.

She pushed his hand away. 'I'm only asking because I'm curious,' she said doggedly. 'Your single status doesn't seem to sit comfortably with a man who adores his country, but who seems to care more about the bloodline of his horse than his own. And I can't work out why that is.'

'Maybe you're not supposed to.'

'But I want to.'

Saladin didn't speak for a moment. This was intrusion, unwanted and unwarranted—a question she had no right to ask. Yet something tugged at him to tell her, and he couldn't work out what that something was. Was it an instinct she possessed—the same instinct that made angry and injured horses respond to her, which perhaps she extended to humans?

He hesitated, feeling the momentary sway of his defences as she surveyed him with that air of quiet stillness and determination. Was this why Burkaan had let her pet him, why his viciousness and pain had been temporarily forgotten in her company—because she exuded an air of healing reassurance, despite her occasional spikiness? He told himself not to confide in her, because keeping his own counsel wasn't just a matter of privacy, it was one of power. The unique and lonely power of a monarch who must always stand apart from other men.

But suddenly the weight of his guilt and his own dark secret felt heavy—too heavy a burden to carry on his own, and for the first time in his life he found himself sharing it.

'Because I have already been married,' he said.

She was shocked; he could tell. For all her bravado in saying this was just about sex, it wasn't that simple. It never was. Not where women were concerned. They always had an agenda; they were conditioned by nature to do so. They always wanted to bond with a man, no matter how much they tried to deny it. He watched as she tried to cultivate just the right blend of nonchalant interest, but he could see that her eyes had darkened.

'Married?' she said unsteadily. 'I had no idea.'

'Why should you? It happened a long time ago, when I was very young—in the days before these wretched twenty-four-hour news channels existed. Those distant days when Jazratan was a country without the world looking over its shoulder.'

'And your…wife?'

He could hear the tentative quiver in her voice. What did she expect him to say—that Alya was locked up in a tower somewhere, or that she was just one of a number of wives he kept hidden away in a harem while he entertained his foreign lover?

'Is dead.'

She didn't respond at first. If she'd come out with some meaningless platitude he probably would have got out of bed and left without saying another word, because nothing angered him more than people trying to trivialise the past. Instead, she just waited—the same way he'd seen her wait when Burkaan angrily stamped his hooves in his box before letting her approach.

'I'm so sorry,' she said at last, her voice washing like cool, clear balm over his skin.

'Yes,' he said flatly.

'She…she had something to do with the Faddi gate and the rose garden, didn't she?' she asked tentatively.

He nodded, but it was a moment before he spoke. 'She was designing it to celebrate our first wedding anniversary, only she never got to see its completion. I had landscape designers finish it, strictly adhering to her plans, but…'

'But you never go in there, do you?' she said, into

the silence that followed his words. 'Nobody does. It's always empty.'

'That's right,' he agreed.

Perhaps it was the fact that she said nothing more that made Saladin start telling her the story, and once he had started the words seemed to come of their own accord—pouring from his lips in a dark torrent. Maybe because it was so long since he'd allowed himself to think about it that he'd almost been able to forget it had ever happened. Except that it had. Oh, it had. He felt remorse pierce at his heart like tiny shards of glass, and following remorse came the guilt—always the guilt.

'Alya was a princess from Shamrastan, and we were betrothed when we were both very young,' he began. 'Our fathers wanted there to be an alliance between two traditionally warring countries and for a new peace to settle on the region.'

'So it was—' she hesitated '—an arranged marriage?'

His eyes narrowed and he felt a familiar impatience begin to bubble up inside him. 'Such an idea is anathema to Western sensibilities, is that what you're thinking, Livvy?' he demanded. 'But such unions are based on much firmer ground than the unrealistic expectations of the romantic love. And it was no hardship to be married to a woman like Alya, for she was kind and wise and my people loved her. She was beautiful, too—like a flower in its first flush. And I let her die,' he finished, the words almost choking him. *'I let her die.'*

She tried to touch him but he shook his head and rolled away from her, turning to stare at the flicker of shadows on the walls—as if it were a betrayal to even look at her while he was speaking of Alya.

'What happened?' she said, from behind him.

He could hear the thunder of his heart as he dragged his mind back to that terrible morning—and, despite his having locked it away in the darkness, the memory seemed as vivid and as painful as ever. 'I had to leave at dawn,' he said heavily. 'For I was due to ride to Qurhah to negotiate with the sultan there, and I wanted to get away before the sun was too high.' He swallowed. 'I could have flown—or even driven—but I wanted to visit some of the nomadic tribes along the way and it is better to take a camel or a horse into these regions, for they are still suspicious of modern transport. I remember Alya waking up just before I left, because she always liked to say goodbye to me. She was screwing up her eyes against the morning light, but we had been awake for some of the night and I thought she was just tired.' His voice cracked. 'So when she complained that her head ached, I told her to go back to sleep and to see how she felt when the maid came to wake her for breakfast.'

'Go on,' she said.

He stared straight ahead. 'I remember she smiled at me and nodded, looking at me with all the trust in the world as I bent over to kiss her. She told me to take care in the desert. And that was the last time I saw her alive.' His words ground down to a painful halt, because even now they were hard to say. 'Because when her maid came to rouse her, she found Alya lying dead.'

'Dead?'

He heard the shock in her voice and he turned over to see that same shock reflected on her face. 'Yes, dead. Cold and lifeless—her beautiful eyes staring sightlessly at the ceiling. Struck down by a subarachnoid haemorrhage at the age of nineteen,' he said, his voice shaking with loss and rage and guilt. 'Lost to us all and let down by the one man who should have saved her.'

'Who?' she questioned. 'Who could have saved her?'

He shook his head incredulously. 'Why, me, of course!'

'And how could you have done that, Saladin? How could you have possibly saved her?'

He clenched his fists together, so that the knuckles turned bone white as they lay against the sheet. 'If I'd thought about *her*, instead of being wrapped up in my own ambition. If I hadn't been so full of triumph about the impending agreement with Qurhah, I might have realised the severity of the situation. I should have delayed my trip and called the doctor, who would have been there by the time she started to vomit copiously. I might have been able to help her, instead of being halfway across the desert when news reached me.'

'You don't know that,' protested Livvy. 'That's pure conjecture.'

'It's fact,' he snapped. 'I could have taken her to hospital.'

'And all the intervention in the world still might not have helped,' she said. 'But you'll never know—because that's just the way life is sometimes. We have to accept that we have no control over it. You have to cherish all the beautiful memories you had with Alya and let go of the bitterness and the blame.'

'Oh, really?' He gave a bitter laugh. 'So suddenly you're an expert on relationships, are you, my little virgin horse whisperer?'

She flinched a little as if she had only just registered the harshness of his words. 'It's always easier to diag-

nose someone else's problems rather than your own,'
she said stiffly. 'And presumably you told me all this
because deep down you wanted my opinion.'

He wasn't sure *why* he had told her. He wondered
what had possessed him to open up and let her see
his dark heart. Was it to warn her off the tenderness
that had started to creep into their nightly lovemaking,
even though he had warned her against such tenderness at the very beginning? And now he regretted his
impetuous disclosure. He wanted to rewind the clock.
To take back his words—and his secrets—so that she
would become just another anonymous woman in his
bed. So what inner demon prompted him to voice his
next question? 'And what is your opinion?'

Livvy sucked in a deep breath, knowing that what
she wanted to say required courage, and she wasn't
sure she had enough within her—not in the face of so
much sudden hostility. Yet wasn't it better to live your
life courageously? To face facts instead of hiding away
from them? Saladin might be a sheikh who ruled this
wealthy land, but in this moment he needed the words
of someone who wasn't prepared to be intimidated by
his position and his power. Who would tell it the way
it was—not the way he wanted to hear it. She drew in
a deep breath. 'You once accused me of allowing the
fact that I'd been jilted to affect my life negatively—
and you were right. But haven't you done exactly the
same with Alya?'

His eyes narrowed. 'What are you talking about?'

She licked her lips. 'Aren't you in danger of using
your wife's death as an excuse to stop you from living properly, in the here and now? She died when you

were newlyweds...' Her voice faltered for a moment as she met the angry glint in his black eyes, but she'd started now. She'd started and she had to finish. 'She was young and beautiful and time hadn't tarnished your perfect relationship in any way—'

'And you're saying it would have done?' he demanded hotly. 'That all relationships are doomed to end in failure or misery? Is that your Western view of marriage?'

'That's not what I'm saying at all. Nobody knows what would have happened,' she said fiercely. 'Because nobody ever does. All I know is that you seem to be letting your unnecessary guilt hold you back.'

'And what if I don't think it's *unnecessary*?' he bit out. 'What if I feel it is the burden I must carry until the end of my days?'

'Then, that's your choice, because nobody can change your mind for you, Saladin. Only you.' She hesitated because this bit was harder. 'Though maybe you prefer it this way. Your lovely wife was cut off in her prime and nobody else is ever going to be able to live up to her, are they? She was perfect in every way, and she always will be because you've put her on a pedestal. And no living woman can ever compare to Alya.'

His eyes narrowed with sudden perception and slowly he nodded his head. 'Ah,' he said tightly. 'Now I understand.'

She was alerted to the dark note that had entered his voice, and her head jerked back. 'Understand what?'

He gave a short laugh. 'Self-regard disguised as advice. Isn't that what you're doing?'

'I'm afraid you've lost me now. I was never very good at riddles.'

His mouth hardened into a cynical line. 'Oh, come on, Livvy. You must know what I'm saying. You seem to have settled very well here in Jazratan. Even my advisors have commented on how well you have fit in. Unobtrusive, modest, yet supremely hard-working—you put to shame our enduring stereotype of the Western woman as a hard-living party animal. Of course, nobody but us knows that our nights have become a feast of sensual delights. And that under cover of darkness you become someone quite different—a creature of pure pleasure.' His black eyes became hooded as he looked at her. 'Perhaps you are reluctant to walk away from all that you have found here. Did you look around at my palace and like what you saw—is that it? Did my pure little virgin see herself as the future queen of Jazratan?'

Livvy stiffened as his words shot through her like tiny arrows. He had taken her well-meaning advice and twisted it, making it sound as if she'd been seeking her own happy-ever-after when all she'd been doing was trying to comfort him. He made her sound grabbing and self-serving and *cheap*.

'You dare to accuse me of something so cynical?' she demanded, hot breath clogging her throat.

'Yes, I dare!' he challenged. 'What's the matter, Livvy—have I touched a raw nerve?'

Pushing her hair away from her hot face, she noticed the tremble of her fingers. 'Actually, I find your arrogance and your assumption breathtaking, if you must know, but at least it's made me see things more clearly.' She drew in a deep breath as she wriggled away from him. 'And I'm going back to England.'

He shook his head. 'No, not yet.'

'It wasn't a suggestion, Saladin—it was a statement. I'm going and there isn't a thing you can do to stop me.'

He reached for her then, his hand moving underneath the sheet to slide around her waist, and Livvy despaired of how instantly her body reacted when he touched her. She bit her lip as he began to stroke her and wished he could carry on stroking her like that until the end of time.

'Look, maybe I shouldn't have said those things.' A note of something like contrition entered his voice as he continued with his seductive caress. 'Maybe I was lashing out because I'd told you so much. More than I've ever told anyone else.'

'It doesn't matter what you say to me now. My mind is made up and I'm going,' she repeated, pushing away his hand. 'Because there's no reason for me to stay. You're obviously suspicious of my motives, and that is your prerogative. But I don't want to be hidden away like a dirty secret anymore. Do you understand?'

His face darkened. 'And what about Burkaan?'

Livvy felt her heart plummet as his reaction confirmed what she already knew—that his racehorse meant more to him than anything. Of course it did. When would she ever learn that she was one of those women who fell for the kind of men who would never love her back?

'Burkaan will be fine,' she said. 'He doesn't need me anymore—we both know that. He's got his appetite back and he's no longer vicious with the grooms. The X-ray results are conclusive.' She paused, suddenly realising how much she was going to miss the feisty black stallion. But not nearly as much as she was going to miss his judgemental master. 'The vet told me this morning how pleased he is with his progress—and he'll continue making good progress, as long as you take it slowly. So don't rush him. A month walking, followed by a month trotting. After that, you can try cantering.'

'Livvy—'

'I mean, obviously there's no guarantee he'll ever race again,' she rushed on, desperate to cut him off before he tried another of those appeals, which this time she might not be able to withstand. 'But you should certainly be able to put him out to stud at some point in the future. And now I think it's best if you leave. No. Please don't try to touch me again, Saladin. It will only complicate things. We both know that.'

She saw the incredulity that had narrowed his dark eyes and wondered if anyone had ever ordered him from their bed before, or tried to oppose his wishes. Probably not. But she needed to do this. She needed to put distance between them and she needed to find an inner strength. Because, despite her furious denial that she was hoping for some kind of future with him, wasn't there a part of her that was doing exactly that? A part that had grown closer to this complex and compelling man and wanted to grow closer still, if only he would let her. A part that badly wanted to love him, as she suspected he needed to be loved.

And she couldn't afford to think that way. Because falling for a desert sheikh who was still in love with his dead wife was asking for trouble.

He sat up in bed, the sheet falling away from him. 'You're really asking me to leave?' he demanded.

'I really am.' She forced a smile. 'Think of it as character-building.'

Saladin felt a fury and a frustration racing through his blood as he stared into her stubborn face. Who the *hell* did she think she was, trying to take control like this? She would leave his employment when *he* was good and ready and not a moment before. Yet she enjoyed taking control, didn't she? She had laid down her rules right from the start—not seeming to realise what kind of man she was dealing with—and had expected him meekly to accept them. Well, maybe it was time she realised that he'd had enough of *her* rules and *her* control.

Yes, he had enjoyed her time here—who wouldn't have done? She had entranced and pleased him on so many levels and cared so beautifully for his beloved stallion. But that was all pretty much academic. Because where could this relationship go? Absolutely nowhere—no matter how much he liked her. And wouldn't her infernal refusal to be sublimated by his power and position irritate him after a while?

'You want to go?' he snapped, getting out of bed and picking up his discarded robe. 'Then, go!'

He saw the brief look of alarm in her eyes that she couldn't quite hide.

'Right,' she said uncertainly.

'I'll arrange transport for you tomorrow. You can leave first thing.'

With a sinking feeling of dread, Livvy watched as he pulled the robe on over his naked body and jammed his headdress into place and then stormed across the room. He didn't slam the door behind him, though he looked as if he would have liked to have done.

And she was left in the empty room with the dread growing heavier inside her and all she could think was, what had she done?

CHAPTER THIRTEEN

IT WAS ICY cold back in England after the seductive warmth of the Jazratian sun. Livvy returned to a stack of unopened mail, a cat determined to ignore her and the realisation that she didn't have a clue what she wanted to do with the rest of her life—except that deep down she knew it no longer involved making beds and cooking breakfasts.

She had left Jazratan with a heavy heart—without even a final kiss from Saladin—knowing she had only herself to blame. She had kicked him out of her bed and told him she was returning to England and he had retaliated by angrily telling her to go ahead. Had she really expected the proud sheikh to mount some sort of campaign to get her to change her mind? She kept telling herself that he'd been offering sex, not security or love. And anyone with half a brain could see it was better to get out now, while her heart was still intact.

Unless it was already too late. Hadn't her heart felt crushed when she'd left Jazratan on Saladin's private jet? When, earlier that same morning, she'd crept along to the stables to rub her cheek against Burkaan's thick mane and the stallion had stamped one of his hooves—almost as if he had shared her grief at parting and had known the reason why salty tears were flowing down her face.

Saladin had been courteous when she'd been granted an audience to say a formal farewell to him—in the throne room, where he was surrounded by his powerful advisors and bodyguards. Had he correctly interpreted the silent plea in her eyes that had asked for a moment alone with him—and simply chosen to ignore it? Or had his mind already been on other things?

Either way, he had given her nothing but a brief handshake and a flicker of a smile, accompanied by a few words of thanks—which had only added to her feelings of misery as one of his staff had presented her with a cheque. And she felt as if she'd sold *herself* somewhere along the way.

But she *hadn't*, she told herself fiercely. She wasn't a victim—not anymore. She'd been sexually awoken by a man who had turned out to be an amazing lover. She had been persuaded back onto a horse and had re-alised just how much she loved riding, and she must be grateful to him for that. If she had learned anything it was that you couldn't let yourself live in the past and be dominated by it. Not like Saladin and the beautiful young wife he was unable to forget. And that was the irony of it all—that he didn't follow the same advice he'd so eagerly given her. He could dish it out, but he couldn't take it.

And if she now believed herself to be in love with him, well—she would have to wait for it to pass.

At least Stella—her part-time help—had disposed of the Christmas tree, and the decorations had been returned to the loft. The snow was all melted and the holiday was nothing but a distant memory when Livvy arrived home. All that remained were a few stray mistletoe berries, which had rolled underneath a bureau in the hall and somehow escaped being swept up.

Livvy wrote an email to Alison Clark and her friends saying what a shame it was they'd had to cancel their visit and expressing her hope that they'd enjoyed their Christmas in the London hotel. Unenthusiastically, she looked down at the blank pages of her diary. Could she really face trying to drum up more business for the year ahead? To wipe out most of her summer by clearing up after people, when she'd been doing it for so long? All to maintain a house that just didn't feel the same any more. Her inherited home now seemed like nothing but a pile of bricks and mortar, not something she was tied to by blood. She found herself looking around the rooms with a critical eye. It was just a too-big house that needed redecoration and a family to bring it alive, not some aging spinster who rattled around in the rooms.

'So what was it like?' questioned Stella as they were cleaning one of the bedrooms a few days after Livvy had returned from Jazratan.

Livvy gave the bedspread another tug. 'What, specifically?'

Stella shrugged her generous shoulders. 'You know. Living in the desert.'

Livvy puffed out her cheeks and sighed as she straightened up. 'It was…different.' She hesitated, trying to be objective. Trying to forget the man who was the very heart of the place. The man who made her own heart ache whenever she thought about him. 'It was lovely, actually. Really lovely. The palace itself is unbelievable—and so are the gardens. There's a kind of beauty in all that heat and starkness, and the stars are the brightest I've ever seen.'

'And didn't they feed you?' asked Stella critically. 'You've lost weight.'

'Of course they did. It's just that—' Livvy gave a wan smile '—I didn't seem to have a lot of appetite. It was very…hot.'

No, not because it was hot. Because she'd been so obsessed with Saladin that she'd barely been able to think about anything else. She still couldn't and it was driving her crazy. There was her future to decide, and she was busy obsessing about a man with black eyes and a hard body, who had taken her to those bright stars and back.

And she would never see him again.

'Well, there's a pipe leaking in the red bathroom. Better get it seen to before it brings the roof down,' added Stella, with her customary love of domestic drama.

The plumbing problems distracted her for a while, and then Livvy burned off a load of frustration by picking up the leaves that had gathered in a sodden heap by the front door.

It was after lunch, when Peppa had finally decided to forgive Livvy for going away and had started winding her furry body around her legs at every opportunity, that the telephone rang. Stella bustled along the corridor to answer it, her eyes nearly popping out of her head as she listened to the voice at the other end.

'It's him,' she mouthed.

'Who?' Livvy mimed back.

'The *sheikh*.'

With a tight smile Livvy took the phone and carried

it through to her little study, trying to control her suddenly unsteady breathing as she gazed out at the garden where water was dripping from the bare branches of the trees and the grass resembled a sea of mud. As a reflection of the way she felt, it was perfect. *You need to stay calm*, she told herself. *You need to be strong*. For all she knew, Saladin might just be phoning for a chat to check she'd got home safely. This was probably normal for people who'd briefly been lovers. He might even be wanting to ask her advice about Burkaan. Yes, that was probably it. But she could do nothing about the wild thunder of her heart.

'Hello?' she said.

'Livvy?'

'Yes, it's me.' But as the silken caress of his voice washed over her, some of her forced calm began to trickle away and Livvy realised that she wasn't any good at playing games, or pretending to be friends. Not when she wanted to blurt out how much she missed him. Not when she wanted to feel his arms around her, holding her very tight. She heard the ping of an email entering her inbox. 'What can I do for you, Saladin?'

'Which isn't the friendliest greeting I've ever heard,' he observed drily.

'But I thought that's the way you wanted it. Formal and polite. I thought we'd concluded our business together. I thought we'd said everything that needed to be said. That was certainly the impression I got when I left.' She paused. 'Which makes me wonder why you're ringing?'

At the other end of the line, Saladin stared out at the sky. Why *was* he ringing? It was a question he hadn't wanted to confront and one that instinctively he shied away from answering. He wondered if he could persuade her to return to Jazratan by telling her that his horse was pining for her, which was true.

He suspected not. He sensed that financial inducements would no longer sway her, no matter how much more generous he made his offer. Just as he sensed that pride wouldn't allow her to accept something that could only ever be second best. He sighed. He realised that, for all her newly awoken sexual liberation, Livvy Miller remained a fiercely traditional woman who would not look kindly on the sort of relationship he usually offered his lovers. And the pain in his heart was very real, wasn't it? The question was how far he was prepared to go to be with her.

'I need to talk to you.'

'Talk away. I'm not stopping you.'

'I'm not having this conversation over the phone.'

'And I'm not offering you an alternative,' she answered coolly. 'What do you want, Saladin?'

'To see you.'

'Sorry. No can do.'

'Livvy,' he growled. 'I'm serious.'

'And so am I,' she said. 'You said some pretty tough things to me that last night. You were suspicious and hostile and accused me of all kinds of devious motivations—'

'For which I apologised.'

Only because you had to, thought Livvy. *Only because you had to.* 'Yes, you did. So surely we've said everything that needs to be said. It was a fantastic affair and I'm sorry it had to end that way—but the point is that it had to end some time.' She cleared her throat. 'How's Burkaan?'

'He's fine. Livvy—'

'Look, I've got to go,' she said desperately as she heard another email ping into her inbox. 'Someone's trying to contact me. Goodbye, Saladin, and…take care of yourself.'

She cut the call before she had the chance to change her mind, or to be lulled by a seductive voice into doing something that would only bring her pain.

After Livvy had put the phone down, she sat down at her desk. She wasn't going to make a fuss about it, she thought, even though her heart was crashing painfully against her ribcage, because the pain would go. It might take time, but it would definitely go. She would answer her emails and carry on as normal and rejoice that she'd had the strength to resist him. Her hand hovered over the mouse and her whole body stiffened as she clicked on the first email and began to read…

An hour must have passed before she realised that she hadn't moved and was sitting in total darkness and that Peppa was mewing plaintively by her feet and Stella had long gone. She ought to do something. She ought to feed the cat and…

And what?

Sit there for the rest of the evening thinking about what a *devious bastard* Saladin really was?

Her eyes skated down the rest of the emails. There were two tentative booking enquiries, plus one of those round-robin jokes that one of her school friends always insisted on sending and that she didn't find remotely funny. And a 'Singles Nite' being offered by the local pub. She screwed her eyes up as she looked at the date. Tonight's date.

Print out this voucher for free entry to the Five Bells 'Singles Nite'. Music, karaoke and so much more!

A sudden new resolution flooded through her as, impetuously, she pressed the print button, fed Peppa and then went upstairs to get ready.

She told herself that she was going to stop acting like a startled hermit and get out there and put everything Saladin had taught her into practice. No longer was she going to live like a nun. There was no reason why she couldn't have other relationships—in the same way that there was no reason she couldn't have another career. Defiantly, she applied more make-up than usual, fished out a sparkly top to wear with her jeans and piled her hair into an elaborate topknot so that it wouldn't get wrecked by the wind on the way out to the car.

When she drew up outside the pub, she almost turned around to go home because music was blaring out at a deafening pitch. Inside it was crowded, but at least the noise became less loud when a woman started swaying around on a small stage, tunelessly singing about her intention to survive. There were a few people Livvy recognised from the village, but not well enough to sit with—so she bought herself a tomato juice, told herself that she would drink it up and then go. *Baby steps*, she thought. *Baby steps. You've come out on your own and it hasn't killed you. And although it's pretty dire—next time might be better.*

She found a corner seat and sat there smiling as if her life depended on it. She tapped her feet to the music and tried to look as if she was having a good time and eventually a man about her age wandered over, with a half-drunk pint in his hand. He had thick hair and crinkly blue eyes and he asked if he might join her.

But before she could answer, a silky and authoritative answer came from behind him.

'I'm afraid not.'

Livvy didn't need to hear the deeply accented voice to know it was Saladin. She should have realised he'd walked in because the pub had suddenly gone quiet and even the woman doing the karaoke had stopped singing as she stared at him incredulously. But who could blame her? Powerful olive-skinned sheikhs wearing dark cashmere weren't exactly at a premium around these parts.

Livvy put her tomato juice down on the table with shaking fingers as the conversation all around them took on a sudden roar of interest.

'How did you get here?' she demanded, her heart starting to race. 'You're in Jazratan.'

'Obviously, I'm not. I flew in today and came here by helicopter,' he answered.

Her face remained unwelcoming, but she kept it that way. *Why* had he followed her and *why* was he here on *her* territory, when she was just starting out on a long journey to forget him? 'What do you want?'

'There are three things I want,' he said grimly. 'And the first involves having a conversation, which won't be possible with all this noise going on. So can we go outside, Livvy? Please?'

She opened her mouth to say that she didn't want to go anywhere with him, except that was a blatant lie and she suspected he would see right through it. And he was asking in the kind of voice she'd never heard him use before. But even so…

'It's raining,' she objected.

'You can sit in my car.'

'No, Saladin,' she said fiercely. 'You can sit in *my* car, and you can have precisely ten minutes.'

He didn't look overjoyed at the suggestion but he didn't object as he followed her into the blustery and rainy night. Outside an enormous limousine was parked with a burly bodyguard standing beside it, but Livvy marched straight past it towards her own little car, feeling inordinately pleased at the almost helpless shrug that Saladin directed at the guard.

But the moment he removed a sock from the passenger seat—what was *that* doing there?—and got in beside her, she regretted her decision. Because the limousine would have been better than this. It was bigger, for a start, and there wouldn't be this awful sense of the man she most wanted to touch being within touching range…and being completely off limits.

'So what's the second thing?' she questioned, in a voice that sounded miraculously calm. 'How did you know I was here?'

'I had someone watching your house who was instructed to follow you,' he said unapologetically. 'When I arrived, they told me you were still here. It was at that point that a ball of fur hurled itself out of nowhere and decided to start attacking my ankles.' He grimaced. 'Your cat doesn't like me.'

'Probably not. I got her from the rescue centre.' She shot him a defiant look. 'She was ill-treated by a man as a kitten and she's never forgotten it.'

There were plenty of parallels between the woman and the cat, Saladin thought. Livvy had been ill-treated by a man, too, and it had made her wary. And he hadn't exactly done a lot to try to repair her damaged image of the opposite sex, had he? He had treated her as if she was disposable. As if she could be replaced. And wasn't it time he addressed that?

He looked at her in the dim light of the scruffy little car, his gaze taking in an unremarkable raincoat and the fiery hair, which the wind had whipped into untidy strands that were falling around her face. She was wearing too much make-up. He'd never seen her in such bright lipstick before and it didn't suit her, and yet he couldn't ever remember feeling such a raw and urgent sense of desire as he did right now. Was that because she had shown the strength of character to reject him—to walk away from the half-hearted relationship he'd given her? Because by doing that she had earned his respect as well as making him realise that they were equals.

'I miss you, Livvy,' he said softly.

He saw a flicker of surprise in the depths of her eyes before her face resumed that stony expression.

'The *sex*, do you mean?' she questioned sharply. 'Surely you can get that with someone else?'

'Of course I miss the sex,' he bit out. 'And I don't want to *get it* with anyone else. There are other things I miss, too. Talking, for one.'

'I'm sure there are many people who would be only too happy to talk to you, Saladin. People who would hang on to your every word.'

'But that's the whole point. I don't want someone hanging on my every word. I want someone who will give back as good as she gets.'

'*I want* doesn't always get,' she responded, infuriatingly.

'I miss seeing the magic you worked on my horse,' he continued resolutely. *And on me*, he thought. *And on me.* 'I want you to come back to Jazratan with me.'

It was as if that single sentence had changed something. As if she'd removed the stony mask from her freckly face so that he could see the sudden glitter of anger in her amber eyes. 'And how far are you prepared to go to get what you want?' she demanded. 'How many people are you prepared to manipulate just so that Saladin Al Mektala can get his own way?'

His eyes narrowed. 'Excuse me?'

Angrily, she punched her fist on the steering wheel. 'I've just had an email from Alison Clark, who you probably don't even remember. She was the woman who was due to spend Christmas here with her polo friends, before you decided you needed me in Jazratan. The group who miraculously decided not to come at the last minute and to spend their Christmas in a fancy London hotel instead. A trip *financed by you*, as I've just discovered in an email written by the grateful Alison. So what did you do, Saladin—have your *people* track down these guests of mine and offer them something they couldn't resist, just so that you could whisk me away from Derbyshire?'

He met her accusing stare and gave a heavy sigh. 'They seemed perfectly happy with the arrangement.'

'I'm sure they were. All-expenses-paid trips to five-star hotels don't exactly grow on trees! But it was a sneaky thing to do and it was *manipulative*,' she accused. 'It was just you snapping your powerful fingers in order to get your own way, as usual.'

'Or a creative way of getting you to come to Jazratan, because already I was completely intrigued by you?' he retorted.

'You just wanted me to fix your horse!'

'Yes,' he admitted, in a voice that suddenly sounded close to breaking. 'And in the process, you somehow managed to fix me. You found a space in my heart that I didn't even realise was vacant. And you've filled it, Livvy. You've filled it completely.'

'Saladin,' she said shakily. 'Don't—'

'I must.' He reached out then and took one of the hands that was gripping the steering wheel and pressed it between the sensuous warmth of his leather gloves. 'Every word you spoke was true,' he said quietly. 'I was using my early marriage and my guilt as a block to forming a meaningful relationship with someone else. But I've realised that what I have with you transcends anything I have known before. That we have a truly adult relationship and we are equals. Yes, equals,' he affirmed as he saw her open her mouth to object. 'I'm not talking about the trappings of my kingdom, or the division of wealth. We are equals in the ways that matter. Or at least, I hope we are because I love you, Livvy Miller. And I'm hoping that you love me, too.'

His words were so unexpected that for a moment Livvy thought she must have imagined them and she tried to ignore the excited leap of her heart—shaking her head with a defiance that suddenly seemed as necessary to her as breathing. 'You're still in love with your dead wife,' she said.

'I will always love Alya,' he said simply. 'But what I had with her was so different from what I had with you. She was very young and in complete thrall to me. I was her king, not her equal. And you were right. She was taken at a time when she was perfect, and that's what her memory became to me. My single status became a kind of homage to her, as well as being a safety net behind which I could hide. When I spoke so disparagingly about romantic love, it was because I didn't believe in it, but now I do. I didn't think it could ever happen to me, but now it has.' His black eyes burned into her steadily. 'There are many different types of love, but believe me when I tell you that my heart is yours, Livvy. That I have found my equal in you. And that even though your stubbornness and refusal to do exactly as I say sometimes frustrates the hell out of me, I love you passionately and truly and steadfastly.'

And then Livvy *did* believe him, because it was too big an admission for a man like Saladin to make unless he really meant it. The passion that blazed from his eyes was genuine and the conviction that deepened his voice crept over her skin like a warm glow, but still something held her back.

'And I love you, too,' she said. 'Very, very much. But I'm not sure if I'm going to be able to be the kind of lover you need.'

'And what kind of lover is that?' he asked gently.

'I've pretty much decided that I'm going to sell up and use the money you gave me to start my own stables,' she said. 'I don't have a clue where that might be. And you'll want a mistress, I suppose. I thought I wouldn't be able to tolerate that kind of relationship, but now that I've seen you again I'm beginning to have second thoughts.' She shrugged her shoulders. 'But when I start imagining the reality—I don't know if I can see myself being set up in some kind of luxury apartment so that you can come and visit.'

He frowned. 'So that I can come and visit?' he repeated, in a perplexed voice.

'Whenever you're in the country. Isn't this how these things usually work?'

His answering laugh sounded like the low roar of a lion as he gathered her into his arms and tilted her chin very tenderly with the tip of his thumb. 'I was hoping you might return with me to Jazratan, as my queen. I was hoping you would marry me.'

Her cheeks burned as she met his eyes, remembering the accusations he had thrown at her.

'I know,' he said ruefully. 'But maybe I accused you of being matrimonially ambitious because already it was playing on *my* mind. Because I've realised there is no alternative scenario that I am prepared to tolerate.' He drew in a deep breath. 'So will you, Livvy? Will you marry me?'

And suddenly Livvy had run out of reasons to keep telling herself that this couldn't possibly be happening and that there must be a catch somewhere. Because there wasn't—and when it boiled down to it, Saladin's past didn't matter and neither did hers. Because right then he was just a man with so much love in his eyes, which matched the great big feeling that was swelling up inside her heart and making it feel as if it were about to burst with joy.

'Yes, Saladin,' she said, putting her arms around his neck and holding on to him as if she would never let him go. 'I'll marry you tomorrow if you want me to.'

EPILOGUE

THEY MARRIED TWICE. Once in the quiet stone chapel where Livvy's own mother and father had been wed, and once in a lavish ceremony in Jazratan, attended by world leaders and dignitaries—as well as a sizeable hunk of the horse-racing fraternity.

At first it felt weird for Livvy to see her photo plastered all over the papers, with Saladin holding tightly on to her hand, her filmy veil held in place by a crown of diamonds and rubies and her golden dress gleaming like the coat of a palomino horse.

She settled happily in the country she had quickly grown to love, determined to learn to speak the Jazratian language fluently and to see Burkaan winning the famous Oman Cup. And if people ever asked her how she had managed to adapt so comfortably from owning a B & B in Derbyshire to being the queen of Jazratan, she was able to answer quite honestly. She told them that the grandness of her husband's palace never intimidated her, because wherever Saladin was felt like home. He travelled less than before, and everywhere he went he took Livvy with him—for he was eager to show off his new bride to the world.

Livvy started working in the stables, whenever her

royal role permitted it, and quickly earned herself a reputation among the staff of being gifted and reliable and never pulling rank. She liked to go riding with Saladin when the sun had started to sink low and the sting of the heat had left the day. Sometimes they rode to 'their' oasis, where they made love beneath the shade of the palm trees.

After a gentle campaign she persuaded Saladin to have a ceremony declaring the beautiful rose gardens officially open—and invited Alya's parents, along with her two brothers and their wives, as guests of honour. It wasn't the easiest of meetings—not at first, for there were tears in Alya's mother's eyes as she tied a small posy of flowers to one of the intricate silver coils on the Faddi gates. And yes, Livvy saw tears in Saladin's eyes, too. But Alya's parents were persuaded to bring their grandsons to play there at any time, and afterwards they all sat beneath the shade of a tree, drinking jasmine tea and laughing as the two sturdy little boys toddled around among the scented bowers.

It would be several years before Burkaan would triumph in the Oman Cup and many more before he was put out to stud, and a new foal—the image of his father—was born. But Peppa the cat grew grudgingly to accept Saladin's presence in her mistress's life and found herself happily living in the royal palace, enjoying the way that the staff fussed around her. There was a bit of a shock when it was discovered that she had sneaked out and mated with a stray tom who had been seen lurking around the back of the stables—but she proved herself an exemplary mother of five kittens.

Wightwick Manor was never sold. Saladin decided that the house should be kept as a base for them whenever they wanted to escape the desert heat to enjoy a spell in the English countryside.

'And it is important that any children we may have will grow up knowing and loving their mother's inheritance, because your roots are just as important as mine, *habibi*,' he said, tenderly stroking Livvy's head, which was currently resting upon his bare chest. 'Don't you agree?'

Livvy wriggled a little, changing her position so that she could prop herself up onto her elbow and stare into the enticing gleam of her husband's black eyes. She trailed a thoughtful path over his chest with her finger, circling lightly over the hard muscle and bone covered by all that silken skin, and it thrilled her to feel him shiver. She liked making him shiver.

'I agree absolutely,' she said as he began to brush his hand against her inner thigh and now it was *her* turn to shiver. 'And in fact, that brings me very nicely to some news I have for you.'

His hand stilled and she knew he was holding his breath—just as she'd held hers when she'd surreptitiously done the test that morning. They hadn't actively been *trying*, but she knew that Saladin longed for a child of his own, and she'd been wanting to have his baby since the moment he'd slid that wedding ring on her finger.

'I'm pregnant,' she whispered. 'I'm going to have a baby.'

And suddenly he was laughing and kissing her and telling her how much he loved her, all at the same time. And it was only after a little time had passed that she noticed that his hand was no longer making its tantalising journey up her thigh.

She caught hold of his fingers and put them right back where they had started from. 'Don't stop,' she said.

'Is it safe?'

She danced her lips in front of his. 'Perfectly safe.'

And that was how she made him feel, Saladin realised dazedly. Safe. As if he'd found something he hadn't even realised he'd been looking for. As if she were his harbour, his refuge and his joy. As if the whole world suddenly made sense. He cradled her head in the palms of his hands and kissed her as deeply as he knew how. And thanked the heavens for that snowy Christmas night, which had given him the greatest gift of all.

The gift of love.

* * * * *

A CHRISTMAS VOW OF SEDUCTION

MAISEY YATES

To Dean Winchester, carry on my wayward son

PROLOGUE

THE GIFTS HAD been on parade for the past hour. Shows of wealth from Tirimia being trotted out before King Kairos as though he were a boy and this was Christmas morning. Baskets overflowing with the finest fruits grown in the orchards from Petras's neighboring country. Art and jewelry from the most celebrated painters and silversmiths. But certainly the ambassadors from Tirimia had saved the most spectacular gift for last.

Kairos looked down from his position on the throne at the men who were standing before him, clearly awaiting his awe, and listened as they began to introduce their final treasure, the one they were calling the jewel of their collection.

"This will please you, my king," the man, known as Darius, was saying. "The ultimate in Tirimian beauty and grace, for your palace. For the continued health of relations between Tirimia and Petras. The representation of how far we've come since the revolution. It was bloody, and we cannot erase that history. We can only show we are committed to moving forward."

Darius was speaking of the overthrow of Tirimia's monarchy some fifteen years earlier. Kairos had not been on the throne then, but his father had made sure he'd been well educated in what was happening. At the time, the rebels in Tirimia had even posed a threat to the borders of Petras. Earning back trust between the two nations had been slow. Which was why they had requested an audience with Kairos today. He was the newly installed king, and they were clearly keen to make the most of the clean slate they felt he might offer.

Too bad for them he wasn't easily impressed with baubles. However, they had quite a few natural resources he was interested in, and war was never in the best interest of the nation. Which was why he had granted them the audience. And watched with decreasing patience as they brought forth their offerings.

"As a token of goodwill between our nations," Darius said, a film of oil coating each word, "we present to you Princess Zara."

The doors to the throne room swung open and there, standing in the center of the doorway, flanked by two large men, was a woman. Her hands were clasped in front of her body, bright gold cuffs gleaming from her wrists.

For a moment Kairos wondered if she was bound. Then she began to walk, her hands falling to her sides, and that momentary fear was alleviated. Her hair was long and dark, caught back in a braid that swung with her every step. Her face was decorated with gold paint, dots above her eyebrows, and a few down below her eyes. She possessed a dark, exotic beauty that stoked no fire in him. She was so unlike his cool, blonde wife, Tabitha. The only woman he wanted. The woman who had chosen to skip this very important procession.

He wished, very much, that Tabitha were here to see this. To see him gifted with a woman. He wondered if her blue eyes would burn with jealousy. If they were capable of burning with anything at all.

Very likely, she would simply sit there, passive and unmoved. She might even suggest he take the girl as his own. So little was her esteem for him these days.

He ignored the kick of regret in his stomach.

"There must be some mistake," Kairos said. "I cannot imagine you intend to give me a human being."

Darius spread his hands wide. "We have no need of a princess in Tirimia. Not now."

"So you seek to give her to me?"

"To do with as you please. Preferably, you would take her as a wife. Her dishonor is not our wish. Though, however you intend to use her…it would be an honor in its way."

Another wife. He could think of nothing worse. "I regret to inform you that I already have a wife," Kairos said, regretting nothing of the kind.

"If you do not believe in taking more than one woman in matrimony in this country, we would find it acceptable if you took her as a concubine."

"I have no positions available for a concubine either," he said, hardening his tone.

"We demand security," Darius said. "If we are to open up our borders to Petras, then we demand blood ties. This is the tried-and-true method of obtaining this level of security."

"And here I thought you were a nation moving into the modern era," Kairos said, looking down at the woman whose eyes burned with anger, who radiated energy, but kept silent, her dark head bowed low. "It seems to me that this stands in contradiction to that."

"Our system of government is young, while our country is old. The marriage between tradition and modern reality is, at best, a clumsy one. We must keep our people happy while moving into the future. Surely you can appreciate some of the issues inherent in that."

Kairos felt a smile curve his lips, an idea forming.

Andres. This would be the perfect occupation for him. A perfect bit of revenge that would satisfy the small, mean part of Kairos that had never fully let go of his brother's betrayal. It would also accomplish great things for the country. Vengeance that furthered his cause as ruler was a rare and glorious thing.

"As I said," Kairos spoke, surveying the room, "*I* already have a wife. My brother, however, is most certainly in need of one. She will be just perfect for him."

CHAPTER ONE

RETURNING TO THE palace in Petras was never Andres's favorite thing. He preferred his various penthouses scattered throughout the world. London, Paris, New York. And a beautiful woman to go in each one. He was a cliché, but he was comfortable with it. If only because it was so much fun.

Petras was never half as much fun. It was where his brother, Kairos, used an iron fist, not for the people of Petras, but for Andres himself. As though he were still a boy needing to be taken in hand, and not a man in his thirties.

Invariably, his stays in the palace followed a staid and steady routine. Visits to hospitals and other approved public appearances where his every word was carefully scripted. Stilted dinners with his older brother and his wife, which were as boring as they were uncomfortable; and long nights spent in his vast royal bedchamber *alone*, because Kairos didn't approve of Andres bringing lovers to stay in the hallowed halls of the Demetriou family. Though Andres thought that had less to do with propriety and more to do with the fact that Kairos was out to punish him for his past misdeeds in a million small ways, every day, until he died.

Which made his discovery, upon entering his bedroom, all the more remarkable.

He walked in tearing at his tie—too tight and constricting, like everything here—slamming the door behind him. Then he froze. There, in the center of his bed, knees curled up against her chest, long dark hair cascading loose over her shoulders like spilled ink, was a woman. They both regarded each other for a moment. Then she scrambled to her feet, stumbling backward on the mattress until her back was pressed against the large ornate headboard that had never been any use to him, as he'd never had a woman in *this* bed.

Until now.

Though she had not been invited, neither did she look very excited to be there. Both of those things were a bit of an anomaly.

"Who are you?" he asked. "What are you doing here?"

She tilted her head upward, her expression defiant. "I am Princess Zara Stoica of Tirimia."

Andres knew very well that Tirimia was no longer a monarchy. In fact, the royal family had been driven from the throne during a bloody revolution back when Andres was a teenager. He hadn't been aware there were any survivors, much less a princess who looked slightly more like a bedraggled creature than a woman.

Her bronzed skin was painted with gold, framing her dark eyes and eyebrows. Her lips were a deep shade of red designed to entice, but he had a feeling that allowing himself to be enticed could be a mistake. She looked much more likely to bite him than kiss him. Her hair hung down well past her backside, disheveled as though she'd been in a fight, or thoroughly pleased by a lover.

Because of the bed, it was tempting to imagine the latter. But judging by the expression on her face, it was most certainly the former.

"You seem to have the wrong palace, Princess."

"I do not," she said, her tone stiff. "I am a prisoner in

my own country, and I was brought here as a gift to King Kairos."

Andres's eyebrows shot upward. His older brother wouldn't know what to do with a woman as a gift, even if he *weren't* bound by marriage vows. "In which case you're in the wrong room."

Her expression turned stormy. "He did not wish to keep me. He, in turn, gave me to his brother."

Andres could not process the absurdity of the statement. This woman, was a gift for him? "Are you telling me that you've been regifted?"

She frowned. "I suppose."

Clearly, she didn't see the humor in this. But then, if he were the one being passed around like an unwanted present at a white elephant party, he might be humorless too.

"Would you possibly mind waiting here for a moment?" he asked.

Her expression turned stormier still. "I would not have been here at all if I had any other options. I have nothing to do but wait."

"Excellent." He turned on his heel and walked back out of the room, stalking down the hall, down the curved staircase that led to Kairos's office. He would no doubt find his brother bent over important paperwork, looking grave and serious and not at all like a man who had just given his younger brother a *woman* as a *gift*.

Andres pushed open the door to the office without knocking, and as he had guessed, Kairos was indeed sitting there laboring over work.

"Perhaps you would like to explain the woman in my bed?"

Kairos didn't look up. "Andres, if I were tasked with explaining every woman in your bed, I would never get anything else done."

"You know what I mean. There is a creature upstairs in my chamber."

Kairos looked up. "Oh, yes, Zara."

"Yes. A princess of some kind? She claims she's a prisoner."

"It's a bit more complicated than that," Kairos said.

"Enlighten me."

His brother actually smiled, the expression nearly knocking Andres to the floor. A smile on Kairos's face was a rare sight. "She was given to me by dignitaries from Tirimia."

"That much I gathered."

"As you know, I'm trying to reestablish trade with them. They are our closest neighbor, and being at odds with them is pointless. More than that, it can be dangerous and costly." Kairos's expression turned serious again. "Our father didn't see the point in mending bridges between the two nations. Here I sit, trying to restore Petras to its former glory, and this is one way I can accomplish that."

"By accepting a woman as a gift like she was an expensive watch?"

"Yes, Merry Christmas a few weeks early."

"Did you want me to keep her in my pocket and ask her the time?" Andres asked through clenched teeth.

"Don't be ridiculous. You're going to marry her."

Anger settled like lead in Andres's stomach. "Oh, I see. This is your belated revenge?"

"Again, don't be ridiculous. I've got a country to run. I hardly have time to seek revenge to the detriment of the people. Now, make no mistake, I may enjoy your discomfort a bit, but it is no less necessary that you make this union a reality."

"You have no reason to hold on to your anger where I'm concerned. You're better off with Tabitha than you were with Francesca anyway."

"That," Kairos said, "is debatable."

Andres had never been under the illusion that his brother and his wife were head over heels in love, particularly not given the circumstances surrounding the marriage. But this was the first time he had ever heard Kairos speak negatively about the state of things.

The fact that Tabitha, once his brother's PA, had turned out to be such a suitable queen was one reason Andres had been able to absolve himself of his indiscretion with Kairos's *first* fiancée five years ago in a Monte Carlo hotel suite.

He'd been so drunk that he hadn't remembered what had transpired between himself and Francesca. But there were numerous photos, and some very explicit video footage plastered all over the internet the following day that had left things in a very unambiguous light. Kairos had been forced to call off his marriage, disgraced and humiliated by his fiancée, and his own brother. Kairos hadn't loved Francesca, that much was clear, and his ire hadn't been born out of a broken heart, but out of the sting of public humiliation.

Shortly after, Kairos had announced his engagement to Tabitha, and the royal wedding had taken place as planned, on schedule, with a different bride. Everything neatly swept under the rug, as though it had never happened. Which made it easy for Andres himself to forget the part he had played in the way the dice had fallen.

But if things with Tabitha weren't all that they appeared...

"And what does that have to do with me?" Andres asked.

"I need you married. I need you to help with the relations between Tirimia and Petras. Princess Zara solves both of those issues. You need to grow up and start behaving yourself. I was lenient with you even after the stunt you pulled with my fiancée. I have been very patient until now. While you have continued to whore your way through Europe and the States, I took over the responsibility of running the country."

"So you're saddling me with a woman who seems to be here against her will?"

"You knew you would have to marry someday. This is no surprise to you."

"I figured I might have some involvement in the selection of my bride."

Kairos pounded his hand down hard on the desk. "Men like us never do. You have lived a life sheltered from the responsibility that faces us. I have not had that luxury. I know the reality of it. You marry appropriately. You do not marry for love. Yes, I suppose I should be thankful you spared me the scandal of having to divorce Francesca. But I selected Tabitha in haste and…it is entirely possible we are facing a larger problem than an issue of marital happiness."

"Are you unhappy?"

"I never expected to be happy. Neither do I require happiness." Kairos rubbed his temples. "What I require is an heir. It may have escaped your notice that I don't seem to possess one."

"I assumed you were trying for one."

Kairos curled his fingers into a fist. "We have never used birth control. Five years, and we have never tried to prevent pregnancy. Possibly more information than you would like, but now you know where things stand."

"What is it you are leading up to here, Kairos? I've never been accused of being the smart one. You have to spell things out."

"You may very well be responsible for producing the next in line to the throne. That means you need to marry. You need to marry royalty. Princess Zara is, in fact, royalty."

"You expect me to exit bachelorhood and start producing babies on such short notice?"

Kairos waved a hand. "Don't be so dramatic about it. Just because you marry doesn't mean you have to change your behavior entirely. Certainly you will have to be more discreet."

His brother suggesting something as shocking as carrying on extramarital affairs was surprising, and was almost as shocking as the fact that Kairos was essentially marrying him off. "Are you unfaithful to *your* wife?"

A muscle in Kairos's jaw jumped. "No. I'm simply telling you that things don't have to change all that much. Obviously your marriage will be one of convenience, and as long as you treat her with respect, I don't see why you should have to pledge your fidelity to her."

"I have no practice with fidelity. I would hardly stake my life on it."

"You knew the day would come when you would have to take some responsibility for the nation. That day is now. It's this. Father may have expected you to amount to nothing, but I certainly expect you to carry your weight."

"I had no idea that as the spare, I was required to carry any weight unless you died."

"Unhappily for you, that is not the case. I need you for political reasons, and practical reasons."

Andres looked down at his brother's dark, furious eyes. "If things are so terrible with Tabitha, why don't you divorce her and find a woman who can give you the children you need?"

Kairos laughed, a hollow, bitter sound. "There are certainly some things you will have to learn if you're to be a husband. I can no more cast off my wife because she can't produce children than give a speech in front of for-

eign dignitaries without clothes on. I would be crucified
by the press. I made vows to her, and I intend to keep
them." He didn't sound happy about it, and certainly his
devotion to her had nothing to do with love. That much
was clear. "It's time to atone for your sins, little brother."

Andres was usually quite content in his sins, with no
desire to atone for them at all. Except for Francesca. That
he would take back a hundred times over if he could. Particularly now, with the stark reality of Kairos's marriage
to Tabitha laid out in front of him, he could hardly defend
those actions.

"You're overlooking a very important piece of the equa-
tion," Andres said.

"And that is?"

"She does not want to marry me. That much was clear
when I encountered her in my bedroom. We're holding a
kidnapped woman."

"She has very few alternatives," Kairos said. "I get the
sense that if she goes back to Tirimia she'll be in danger.
For all that their government is playing nicely with us
now, things are far too tentative for me to stake her life
on presumed decency. She is safest here."

"She's feral. What do you expect me to do with her?"

"You're a legendary playboy. The last thing you need
from me is advice on how to deal with women."

"She is not a woman. She's a *creature*."

He thought of that wild dark hair, her glittering, angry
eyes. Somehow they were supposed to make a royal couple? He would need a woman twice as tame as Tabitha to
convince the public of a change in him.

A woman such as her wouldn't make his reinvention
easy.

Kairos laughed, an even rarer occurrence than a smile.
"I'm a married man, but even I noticed there was enough

to recommend her. She's beautiful, though, I confess not overly sophisticated."

"I was too busy being surprised by her presence in my bedroom to notice her beauty." A lie. He was not blind to her curves, her full, sensual lips. Despite the fact that, for all he knew, she might attack him if he approached her, she was a lush little package.

"My word is law," Kairos said, his tone uncompromising. "And you owe me, brother. You will obey me on this. Tame her, train her, *seduce* her, I don't really care, but by God you will marry her."

Andres clenched his teeth together. He would find the moment more surreal if he hadn't long suspected that it was coming. That someday he would stand before his brother and be informed of his fate. He was a prince, the second born to an old royal family. He had never imagined he would escape marriage, children. It had always only been a matter of time. And his time, it seemed, was up.

"Anything else, Your Highness?" Andres asked, his tone dry.

"Don't take too long."

CHAPTER TWO

PRINCESS ZARA STOICA, heiress to no throne at all, was tired of waiting on the whims of men. It was because of men that she had been uprooted from the palace as a child, sent out to live in the deep, dark woods with the nomadic people who inhabited them, kept safe thanks to centuries-old traditions of honor and hospitality. It was men who had stolen her from her safe haven fifteen years later, and elected to use her as a pawn to further political unions with neighboring nations. Of course, it had also been a man sitting on the throne here in Petras who had decided it was perfectly acceptable to keep her and pawn her off on his brother as a sort of postwar bride.

As a result, it was not a terrible surprise that it was a man who clearly owned this room, and who had burst in close to an hour ago, nearly terrifying the life out of her.

It occurred to her that it was entirely possible she had been installed in Prince Andres's room. The man she was supposed to marry. The very idea made her shiver down to her bones.

Worse than fear was the restlessness starting to run through her veins. She was growing bored, closed up here in the bedroom.

There was a view of the city from a small window by the bed. She found no comfort in such a view. Houses clustered together tightly, high-rise buildings beyond that. Cars cluttering up the roads like a line of dizzy ants desperately seeking food. She preferred the crisp, clean air of the mountains. The silence held close around her by thick evergreens.

She had a difficult time marking passing hours while shut up in vast castles with nothing but man-made architecture sprawled out before her.

She flopped backward onto the bed, sinking deeply into the down-filled blankets and soft mattress.

It was shocking, being exposed to such comfort.

Her years spent living in caravans with her caregivers had been cozy, and not uncomfortable, but it had certainly been nothing like this. And when the new political leaders of Tirimia had brought her back to the old palace, they certainly hadn't installed her in anything half as luxurious.

She looked up at the ceiling, at the ornate molding, the large chandelier that hung from the center of the room. She could not recall ever having been in a bedchamber with a chandelier. Tirimia was a much more modest economy than Petras, even before the revolution.

A sense of unease washed over her and she scrambled off of the bed. She did not want that man, whether or not he was Prince Andres, coming in and finding her like that again. It was unsettling. She paced the length of the room—and it was a fairly impressive length—before retracing her steps, pausing at a door that was firmly closed. She wrapped her fingers around the ornate knob and pushed it open, finding a vast bathroom on the other side. It was much more modern than the rest of the room.

There was a large shower in the corner of the room, glass panels closing it off from the rest of the space. There was also a large, sunken tub that nearly made her groan with longing. The very thought of submerging in warm water sent an intense craving through her that rivaled any she'd ever had for a dessert. A long, hot bath was something that was simply impossible out in the middle of the forest, and something that hadn't been afforded her when she was brought back to the palace as a glorified prisoner.

It was a temptation, but if she thought being discovered in a bed that was not her own was humiliating, certainly being discovered in the bath would be worse.

She walked slowly across the room, moving to a large vanity and mirror mounted at the back wall. There were small bottles displayed on the clean marble surface. She wondered what a man did with so many bottles of lotions and scents. She reached out and took hold of one, unscrewing the lid and lifting it to her nose, sniffing cautiously. It was a cologne, smelling of sandalwood and other spices. She tried to remember if the man she had encountered earlier smelled of those things. She could not.

She set the bottle back down, picking up the next one. This one contained lotion, and it was a temptation too far for her. She tipped it cautiously, squirting a small amount onto her hands, before putting the bottle back in its place. She smoothed the thick cream over her hands, luxuriating in the feel. Her skin had grown rough from so many years of hard labor and living outdoors. A sign of strength, she often thought, and she had never regretted it. Still, it didn't mean she couldn't indulge in one small moment of softness.

"What are you doing?"

She turned sharply, backing herself up against the edge of the vanity, knocking several of the bottles over as she did. "I was bored," she said, looking up to see the same man she had encountered earlier standing in the doorway glaring fiercely at her.

The impact of him was beyond that of a physical blow. She was accustomed to large men, men with a commanding presence that pushed you back, held you at a distance.

Some might call the people she had been raised with Gypsies, based on their simple, nomadic lifestyle, but they weren't, not in blood heritage. They were part of a small, mostly destroyed minority group in Tirimia who still clung to the old ways. Not a warrior culture in the traditional sense, but fiercely protective of the camp and of anyone they felt to be under their care.

However, the gruff exterior of the men she had been raised around could not have been more different from the suave, confronting aura given off by this man. One would think that a man in a suit would not be half as intimidating as one in old jeans. This man should have appeared to be vastly more civilized, and yet it was that veneer of civility that she found frightening. Because she sensed so much beneath it. A hidden depth and strength, buried so deep she had no way of assessing it.

She didn't like this at all. Didn't like the fact that she was in the dark about so many things. At home, things had been so much simpler. She had been protected. She had been certain of her surroundings. The world had been small, containing the forest, her caravan, the cooking fires and people she had known for most of her life.

There were rules. And she had been certain in them.

Now she was here. In a strange land, confronted by a stranger.

A large, broad-chested stranger in a well-cut suit. With short black hair, a square jaw and strong, dark eyebrows. He was beautiful in the same way a predator was. Lethal, and difficult to look away from. She had never, in all her life, been held captive by a man in such a way. So far the men she encountered could easily be divided into two categories. Those she had grown up with and seen nearly every day of her life, and those she considered an enemy.

This man was neither, and that made him unique.

She might yet decide he was an enemy, but for now, she would hold off on that assessment. He might well be dangerous, but he could also very well be her only ally. She had realized two months ago, when she was kidnapped from the encampment, that she had only a spare few options. If she tried to escape her captors and go back to the clan, they would be punished. A poor repayment for shared food, clothing and shelter of the past fifteen years.

Escaping and staying in Petras was no more of a possibility.

She had no money, no form of identification. She didn't know the layout of the city, or of the country beyond. She couldn't drive, and she had no friends.

She would have to make one.

Zara eyed the man standing in the doorway of the bathroom. She wondered if she could make a friend of him. Well, not a friend. Not in the true sense.

But it would do no good to battle him all the way. She would need to be compliant, to a degree. To watch for the right moment to make her move. Whatever it might be.

"You were bored?" he asked, repeating her words back to her.

"Yes, I don't know how long I've been in here, but it has been quite a while."

"Perhaps we should start over," he said. "I am Prince Andres. It appears we are to be married."

Unease, followed by a rash of unexplainable heat coursed through her veins. "Is that so?"

His words confirmed her suspicions. That he was the owner of this room. That he was now the owner of *her*.

"I am informed." He arched one dark eyebrow. "Perhaps you would like to continue this discussion in a more comfortable setting?"

She nodded slowly and began to walk toward him. Then her stomach growled, the sound echoing in the space. "I'm hungry," she said. She realized then that she hadn't eaten since very early this morning.

"Then I will arrange for you to be fed."

It didn't take long for Andres to procure the promised food. He had a tray of meats, cheeses, fruits and breads sent up to the bedroom, which was how Zara found herself sitting on the bed again, her legs covered with a blanket, eating the spread that had been placed before her.

She could feel his watchful gaze on her as she ate in near silence. He hadn't interrupted her yet, but she could see that he wanted to. For the first time in a very long while she felt she might have the upper hand. A very *slight* upper hand, to be sure, but he seemed nearly as confused and put off by the entire situation as she was. Which was, in her estimation, why he was being so watchful. And why he was letting her eat undisturbed. He was circling her, as though she were a potentially dangerous creature and he was concerned about being bitten.

The thought sent a pleasurable rush of power through her, joining the sated sensation in the pit of her stomach brought about by the cheese. Her needs had always been simple. At least, they had become simple once she was sent to live with the nomads at just six years old. They had been simple by necessity. But lately, her needs had shrunk down even further. Warmth, food, shelter. If she had those things, she knew she could keep on going.

Good food and *soft* blankets were several notches more extravagant than she'd had in the past couple of months. And a bit of power? Very heady icing on top of this unexpected cake.

So she continued to eat in silence, sensing his growing impatience, allowing it to feed her small, mean satisfaction.

"How long has it been since you were fed?"

His question surprised her. "Since this morning."

"You are too skinny," he said, his tone matter-of-fact. His words offended her, and she couldn't quite figure out why. She had never given much thought to her appear-

ance. The men who had taken her captive had assigned
a woman to make her beautiful for presentation to the
king, but Zara couldn't say it had mattered much to her.
They had put too much makeup on her, the gold around
her eyes her own addition, a nod to the culture she had
adopted as her own. Her beauty had never been a topic
of discussion among the nomads. She had been under the
protection of the leader, Raz, and he had forbidden any
man from touching her, or even looking at her in a dis-
respectful manner.

And now this man was telling her she was too skinny.
And she was angry.

"I will say that my captors did not overly concern themselves with the quality of my food."

"You are a captive?" he asked, his tone fierce.

"I'm surprised you care. Your brother did not appear
to be similarly concerned. He was quick to accept me as
though I were a...a fruit basket."

He looked her over. "You are most certainly not a fruit
basket, that much is evident."

"I have been passed around like one." She sniffed, allowing herself a moment to fully revel in the indignity of
it all. At one time, she had been a princess. A member of
the royal family in Tirimia. Being in a palace such as this
would have been her right. Before she had been wrenched
away from the only home she'd ever known, robbed of her
family. Her birthright. "I suppose I can only be grateful
no one has plucked at any of my grapes and taken small
samples, so to speak."

She looked up and caught his dark gaze, the sharp
shock of heat piercing her straight to her stomach. She
felt her face warm and she looked away. "Indeed, that
would have been a shame. I'm glad your grapes remain...
unsampled."

A muscle beneath her eye twitched. "Remarkable under

the circumstances, I should think." She had spent a great many years being protected, but that did not mean she was ignorant of the ways of men.

"You were the princess in Tirimia," he said, his tone vaguely accusatory.

"I *am* the princess. I have been replaced. Not by another princess, but by a farcical government who pretends to care about the freedom of the people, when, in truth, they only care about their own power."

"I thought the entire royal family was killed during the revolution."

Her insides grew cold. That always happened when she thought of her parents. Of her older brother. Her memories of them were soft around the edges now, worn like old, weathered photographs. But what remained, as sharp and terrible as ever, was the coldness she'd felt when she learned of their fates.

It hadn't been sadness in its simplest form. It had been death itself. A chill that had stolen through her, replaced all of her blood with ice. It had taken months to thaw. Months for her to feel anything at all again beyond the frost that had taken up residence in her chest.

"Obviously I wasn't," she said, the words strange, thick on her tongue. Because they'd never felt right. None of it had ever seemed right. "Everyone else…my mother, father, my brother, they were all killed. My mother's personal maid had family living in the forest, people who practiced the old way of life. And she brought me to them. They have kept me, protected me, for years."

"Until now, clearly."

She picked up a piece of bread and tore a chunk from it. "Obviously not through any fault of their own. They were ambushed and I was kidnapped."

"And can you be returned to them?" he asked.

She weighed that question and all of the possible implications. If she told him yes, would he help her? Or was he intent on…marrying her.

The idea of marriage was ludicrous to her. Foreign. She was not in any way ready, or suited, to be a man's wife. She had no interest in such things.

The very idea was her worst nightmare. Wearing a crown again. Placed on a throne.

A target would be on her back, and she would be up on a pedestal where she was an easy target.

She had lived through that nightmare once. She had no intention of entering into it again.

She should tell him to take her home.

And have the only people on this earth who tried to protect you destroyed?

That bitter, familiar cold lashed at her again. She couldn't go back. It was too dangerous. It was selfish. They would protect her with their lives, and it was very likely their lives would, in fact, be the cost.

She had lost too much already. Too many people who had believed deeply in their convictions cut down. To hear Raz speak of her parents, her father had been a man of conviction. Who had fought to change antiquated ideas in Tirimia, who had made a pact with Raz's tribe to preserve their sovereignty within the nation.

For that, he had been killed. Out of loyalty and respect to her father, Raz had risked the tribe to protect her, to raise her.

She wouldn't put them at risk again.

This was something she would have to figure out on her own. She would have to rescue herself.

"No," she said. "I cannot be returned to them. It would be far too dangerous."

"Wonderful," he said, his tone at odds with the word.

"I will not be marrying you, of course," she said, taking a grape from the platter and holding it between her thumb and forefinger.

"Is that so?" he asked.

She nodded, keeping her expression grave. "I have no desire to marry."

"Why is that?" he asked, reaching out and plucking the grape from her fingers. "Concerned over having your grapes sampled?" He put the fruit in his mouth and she found herself transfixed, trying to untangle the wealth of meaning in his words while watching his lips, his jaw, work slightly as he chewed.

Why was the way he chewed interesting? It shouldn't be. She'd never found chewing fascinating in her life.

"I don't know you," she said, looking away and picking up another grape, biting into it with no small amount of fierceness. "And that's just for a start."

"We have nothing but time to work this out. You could list your reasons. Extensively."

"I won't have a complete list until I know you better."

"I think what you just described *is* marriage. Two people who truly don't know each other and are somewhat blind to each other's faults until time and proximity force them to really get a good look at the poor choice they made."

"You make it sound so appealing," she said, shifting her position, tucking her feet beneath herself and leaning forward, taking a piece of fig from the platter.

"I'm not a great believer in the institution."

"Then why should we marry?" she asked.

"Because," he said, his tone weary, "my brother has said it shall be, and so it shall be. There are a great many perks to being the spare in the royal family, Zara. Not the least of which is that I have been able to cast the mantle of responsibility off for the past thirty-two years with very few consequences. While Kairos has always been bound by duty, honor and all manner of other words that make me feel like I'm about to break out in hives. The downside," he added, leaning in, studying the platter, but not taking any more food, "is that I am also beneath his rule." Andres looked up then, his dark eyes meeting hers. He was close now. So very close.

And he did, in fact, smell like the cologne she had found in the bathroom.

"I see," she said, barely able to force the words out past her constricted throat. "Are you going to tell me you're a prisoner too?"

He straightened and she nearly sighed in relief. For some reason, having him so close to her was disturbing in ways she couldn't quite work out.

"No," he said, "I'm not a prisoner. Just a prince. That means there are certain expectations I'm obligated to fulfill. Make no mistake, I've spent the past decade and a half steeped in debauchery and generally ignoring all of my responsibilities. We all have to face a reckoning, eventually. You are mine."

Arrogant. That was what he was. To sit there and call her his reckoning when she'd been dragged here against her will. To speak of his duty as such a burden when her father had lost his life upholding the crown in Tirimia, fighting for what was right.

What did this man do with his position? Nothing, from the looks of things.

"You speak of being a prince with such disdain. I am a princess, forced into hiding because of the title. My parents were killed because they were royalty, and yet you stand here, perfectly whole, complaining of being forced into marriage by your brother. How terribly sorry I am for you that your life of extended pleasure is being interrupted by duty. My parents died for duty."

"Am I supposed to regret that that isn't an option fo

me? Should I go offer my neck to the guillotine rather than
my hand in marriage?"

"My parents are dead," she hissed.

"And I am sorry. But I am not sorry that I don't face
the same peril. This is not the same country, nor am I in
the same position."

"You have your life and your opportunities and still
you speak with such disrespect of the position."

"And still, you will be my wife."

"Never," she hissed, knowing that now, with hair
tousled and her posture mirroring that of an angry cat,
she was looking every inch the feral creature he clearly
thought she was.

"What are your options, *agape*?" he asked, the endear-
ment strange to her ears. "You said yourself you cannot
return home. Where will you go if you don't stay here
with me?"

Words churned through her mind, but when one would
rise to the surface, it would slip back beneath just as
quickly, before she could grab hold of it.

"Nowhere," he said, answering for her. "You can speak
of life and death all you want, as though it is all that matters, but here in this position you see that. There are many
shades of gray within living and death, and unhappiness
through a forced marriage is most certainly one of them.
But you're like me. You've hit a wall. You have no choice."

"There is always a choice," she said, not sure where the
words came from, but certain, even as she spoke them,
that they were true. "I live because of that truth. Because
rather than giving up, my mother's maid chose to save
me. Because rather than sending me back, the clan chose
to care for me. We always have choices."

"I suppose you're right," he said, his dark gaze far too
assessing. "Then this is my choice, and I'm making it.
I owe my brother a debt, beyond the typical royal duty.

I'm in no position to refuse his demands. And I choose to obey them."

"What of my choices?"

"They are somewhat crippled in this situation. I won't lie."

"Crippled? They are completely incapacitated."

He shrugged as though he were pushing her protests of his shoulders. "Perhaps. But this is the reality. Whether you want to or not, you, Princess Zara Stoica, will be my wife by Christmas."

CHAPTER THREE

"Prince Andres."

Andres looked up, at the servant who was standing in the doorway of his brother's study, the other man's expression concerned. Andres and Kairos had spent the evening playing cards and drinking Scotch. Possibly both avoiding the women in their lives.

Andres still had a hard time believing he *had* a woman in his life in any capacity other than his bed. In addition to the fact that she was his fiancée and not simply a lover, he did not want her in his bed. Not now.

He could no more imagine bedding that creature than he could imagine willingly sticking his hand into a badger den. Just another reason he'd tasked his brother's staff with placing her in a different wing of the palace.

He had spent the earlier part of the night discussing the marriage with Kairos. And Kairos's expectations. Of course, they would be figureheads for the nation. Actively involved in political and social events. A counterpart to himself and Tabitha, particularly important since it could potentially be up to them to produce heirs.

That meant they had to be at least half as respectable as Kairos and Tabitha, a feat Andres couldn't imagine either of them managing.

A concern only deepened by the very worried look on the servant's face. "Princess Zara refuses to be moved."

Andres dropped his cards onto the table in front of him. "What do you mean she *refuses*?"

The man cleared his throat. "She was quite...adamant. She says she is comfortable."

Kairos made a dismissive noise. "Unsurprising. She is already unwilling to leave your bed." Kairos sounded... envious. Kairos had it very, very wrong.

"That is not it," Andres said darkly.

Kairos raised an eyebrow, and Andres recognized his own features looking back at him. It was rare that he saw the similarities between himself and his brother, but he saw them now. "My wife quite happily has her own room."

"Mine most certainly will," Andres said, his voice a growl. "Perhaps a gilded cage is in order. One with a very firm lock." He sucked in a sharp breath. "I don't know how you expect me to make a princess of her."

"She is a princess," Kairos said, his tone bland.

"You know what I mean."

"I thought, perhaps, it might cost you so much energy to tame her that you might tame yourself in the process."

Andres glared at his brother, anger roaring through him. If only Kairos weren't so far from the truth. It was the very idea of managing to tame both of them that made it seem so impossible. He said nothing else. He stormed toward the door, and the servant stepped out of his way.

"If you cannot remove her," Andres tossed back as he walked down the hall, "I will do it myself."

He walked to the staircase, taking the marble steps two at a time before striding down the hall toward his chambers. He pushed the doors open and was met with an empty room.

His future bride was nowhere to be seen. He stalked through the room and approached the bathroom, flinging the doors open wide.

He heard a squeak, then a splash. He looked toward the bath where he saw a very wet, indignant woman.

"What are you doing in here?" she demanded, as though she were the royalty in the room.

He supposed, in all fairness, she was one part of the royalty in the room. However, the only thing she had ever ruled over was a campfire, if the information he had received on her background was correct.

"This, *Princess*," he said, his tone hard, "is *my* bathroom, in *my* bedroom. You were asked to move. It was brought to my attention that you refused."

"I am comfortable here," she said, sinking farther beneath the water, her expression stormy, her actions proving her words to be a lie. She was anything but comfortable, at least at the moment.

"What a terrible coincidence. I find that I am also comfortable here. As it is my room, with all of *my* things."

"I was brought here against my will," she said. "I am out of my element. I am frightened."

Anger fired through him. He wasn't sure why his reaction was so out of proportion with what was happening. It would cost him nothing to sleep in another room, and yet he found he couldn't let this go. Probably because Kairos was already maneuvering him as though he were a marionette. He had no choice but to allow that, as Kairos was the king here in Petras. However, he did not have to let this little *creature* maneuver him too. And he would not. If she was to marry him, then she would need to understand that he was not to be trifled with.

He had a reputation as a playboy in the media, as the more laid-back half of the two Demetriou brothers. But that only held as long as he went untested. As he was a prince, very few people had attempted to test him. But Zara seemed intent on doing so, and he could not allow it.

"I do not believe you are frightened," he said, moving nearer to the bathtub.

She lowered herself deeper beneath the surface of the water, until her chin was submerged, her large, dark eyes pinned on his. "Of course I am. You are very large. Much larger than I am. You have invaded my space."

"Begging your pardon, Princess," he said, moving closer to the bath, bracing his hands on the edge of the marble tile and leaning in. "It is you who have invaded my space. I did not invite you here. I did not get down on bended knee and propose to you, nor did I at any point surrender my own personal space to you for your continued use."

She squirmed, and he could see her crossing her legs beneath the water, raising her arms to cover her breasts as best she could. The details of her body were indistinguishable as it was, and her belated show of modesty only drew attention to that which she was trying to hide.

She was beautiful. He could not deny that. Acres of smooth golden skin, wide, dark eyes that were just as pronounced now with all her makeup washed off as they had been when they were rimmed with black and gold. Her lashes were long and thick, her lips full, her cheekbones high, giving her a proud, sensual look that would certainly turn heads wherever she went.

When it came to appearance, she was everything he might have wanted in a wife, in a princess. It was her manner that left much to be desired. In fact, her manner left everything to be desired.

He had not often thought of what sort of woman he might take as his wife, because he had put off thoughts of a wife, even though he knew he would someday take one. Still, in the back of his mind he had thought he would probably marry a woman who exuded a kind of serene sophistication. One who would make his life easier. The perfect accessory to all events. As necessary and yet understated as a nice pair of cuff links.

Zara was no more a cuff link than she was a fruit basket.

"I'm distressed," she said, her tone growing more arch by the second. "I was rooted out of my home only two months ago, held prisoner in the palace—"

"So I have heard. And while I do possess a small amount of sympathy for you, I am unsure what you expect me to do about it. You said yourself, I cannot return you to your family. You do not wish to marry me. You have told me that, as well. So here I have a short list of the things you cannot do, and the things you do not wish to do. If you could tell me one thing that you *do* want, that might be of greater use to me than hearing everything I am unable to do."

"I find myself quite comfortable in this room, in this bath, at least I was until I acquired your company. With that in mind, perhaps you might let me stay here, as it is somewhat familiar."

"Are you so fragile that moving down the hall will disrupt your sensibilities?"

"I am quite fragile!"

He had a feeling that, had she been standing on dry ground, she would've stamped her foot to add punctuation to the statement.

"You are a great many things, but I would not characterize you as fragile."

"Leave me," she said, issuing orders like a queen.

"No," he said, "I think not."

He reached beneath the water, uncaring if the sleeves of his shirt were soaking wet. He wrapped one arm around her shoulders and the other beneath her knees, straightening, holding her naked and dripping wet against his chest. He did not look at her, keeping his eyes fixed straight ahead as he strode from the bathroom back into the bedroom.

"What are you doing?" She began to squirm, surprisingly strong, and difficult to maintain a hold on as she did.

She was also, he noticed, very soft. Soft to the touch, soft the way a woman should be.

And joining the flame of anger in his stomach was a sudden burst of arousal that took him completely off guard. He tamped it down, ignoring it, his teeth clenched tightly together as he fought the temptation to look down at her naked body.

This was not about sex. It was about reclaiming the territory that she had attempted to stake as her own.

If he was to marry this little devil, he would have to show her that he would have the upper hand. That she would not be dictating to him.

That went for his body, as well.

He had to take utter control, of her, of himself. There was no other option. He would have to be firm with her. Starting now.

"Let us get one thing straight," he said. "This is not a hotel. This is my bedroom. This," he added, tossing her down with no gentleness whatsoever onto the center of his bed, "is my bed. I do two things in this bed. I have sex and I sleep. If you intend to *stay* in my bed, you will partake in both of those things with me. Otherwise feel free to find a more suitable accommodation."

Again, he resisted the temptation to look at her body, though he imagined she was currently spread out for him like a particularly delectable buffet. But he intended to scare her off, not violate her in any way.

She wasn't still for long. She scrambled across the mattress and buried herself beneath the blankets, shielding her body from his view. "You," she said, her voice shaking, "are terrible."

"We are to be married," he said. "Nothing I've done or said should be all that shocking." He knew full well he was being shocking; he just didn't care.

"I don't know you."

"But you will know me quite well in only a couple of months' time. We could start now."

"We shall not!"

"Then you shall vacate my bedroom. I find that I am quite tired." He reached up, grabbing hold of the knot on his tie and loosening it.

Her eyes went wide, her hands curling tightly around the white comforter on his bed, digging sharply into the material like claws. "You wouldn't," she said, her shocked tone spurring him on all the more.

He kept his eyes on hers as he tugged his tie off and cast it to the floor before undoing the top button on his shirt. "As I said, I find I am quite tired. This is my bed. I have already given you the list of activities performed therein."

He undid a second button on his shirt and watched as her eyes grew even rounder. He undid another, then another, moving closer and closer to the bed. He found his own heart was starting to pound harder. He would not touch her. He knew this would end with her running away before he had to. Still, that didn't stop the blood from firing harder and faster through his veins.

His mind might be well aware that he was a modern man who would never take advantage of a woman in such a way, but his body clearly hadn't gotten the memo. All he knew was that he was a man, and she was a woman. A very beautiful woman.

And in that moment he started to forget exactly what he was doing here.

He undid yet another button on his shirt, and suddenly she rolled to the side, wrapping the blanket around her body and landing on the floor. She stood up, the blankets concealing her curves. Her dark hair was wet, stringy and partly covering her face. And with all that, she was still trying to look imperious. "All right. You may arrange separate quarters for me." She turned to the side, kicking the excess fabric from the comfort her out of her way. "I am going to dress. When I return I expect for things to be arranged."

He laughed at her retreating form, and her shoulders grew stiff, her frame all but vibrating with rage.

He took his phone out of his pocket and made a call to his brother's chief of staff, letting him know that the princess was ready to be shown to her room. Zara returned before the staff came to escort her away. She was dressed in a pair of soft pink pajamas that looked as though they belonged on a much younger, much less venomous girl.

"Am I leaving soon?" she asked.

"Listen to you. Quite impatient to go now."

"You make a very persuasive argument."

He chuckled again, amusement at her open hostility irresistible. He was not used to this reaction from women. But then, he was not used to being engaged to a woman. A woman who clearly didn't want to be engaged to him any more than he wanted to be betrothed to her. "Most women don't run away from me when I start taking my shirt off."

Her lip curled. "I am not most women, you will find."

He rubbed his chin, eyeing her figure, certainly not displayed to any advantage by the flannel she was currently wearing. "This may be a problem, as I expect you to be very like a woman when it comes to our marriage. You must be both a wife to me and a suitable public display for my country." And he had to be the prince his brother needed him to be.

"I am unsuitable," she said, far too quickly.

"And yet my brother says you *are* suitable. The only suitable choice, in fact. So there we have a problem." He regarded her even more closely. Her dark eyes were glittering, and for the first time he saw that there was quite a deep well of fear beneath her prickly exterior. For the first time he questioned the way he had handled her. He was angry at being maneuvered, and he was taking his anger out on her. But she was not a part of this, any more than he was. "You have nothing to fear from me. You have nothing to fear from Kairos, even though he can come across as quite the tyrant. Neither of us is going to hurt you."

He saw no signs of relief on her face. "But you are going to use me," she said.

"You are royalty, Zara. Had you not been thrown out of the palace as a child and spirited away to live with the Gypsies, you would certainly be facing an arranged marriage anyway. Just as I expected I would be one day, though not quite with such short notice."

"Don't you dare lecture me on the responsibility of royalty. My life as a royal was stolen from me."

"And here you have it back. The price of admission into the life is marriage."

"I did not expect it," she said, her tone stiff.

"Did you ever expect to marry?"

She blinked. "I'm only twenty-one."

"Not so young in your country. So I ask you again, did you ever expect to marry?"

She lifted her shoulder. "Were I a typical part of the clan I was raised in, I would likely be married by now. But I was not. I was under their protection. So different things were expected."

"Is that your very long, uninteresting way of saying you did not expect to marry?"

Her expression darkened. "I may have someday. But I was in hiding to spare my own life, in order to save myself from a fate such as this. I hadn't given it much thought. I knew I would have to leave if I was ever going to pursue a normal existence…"

"I suppose this isn't exactly normal."

"Indeed."

"You will need to be trained," he said.

Her frown deepened. "Oh, really?"

"Yes. I think it's entirely possible for you to be made into a suitable bride. You have the looks for it. You simply need…taming."

"Am I so wild?"

"You have no sense of decorum. Your burrowing into my room is evidence of that. Your hair, your posture… You exude."

"I exude what?"

He let out a long, slow breath. "You exude. In general that isn't something a princess should do. You need to be…placid. Serene. As I said before, tame."

She clenched her hands into fists, her expression filled with rage. Her dark hair hung lank down her back, making her look all the more wild. "I refuse to be tamed."

He wasn't entirely sure what to say to that, and he resented her for making him feel as if his back were up against a wall. Kairos had given his orders, and Andres had sins he needed to atone for.

Part of him wondered why he was making an effort. He failed, that was what he did. Their father had always been quick to remind him of that fact when they were boys, and still when they were men. Kairos was the responsible one, the heir, thankfully, as he took his role so very seriously. Andres had been the one his father could always count on to create a scandal, to make a mess, to create disaster.

There was a reason he'd been barred from official events as a child. Reasons he had spent state dinners locked in his room while the rest of the family put on a show.

Their father might be dead now, but the feel of his cold

eyes on Andres remained. Of the hard disappointment that had laced every word the old man had ever spoken to him.

He had given Kairos his word, and he would not fail. Not again. In this, he would triumph.

It was only marriage. And she was only a woman. How could he lose?

He was a legendary playboy renowned for his skills of seduction. Surely he could seduce this scraggly waif easily enough.

"You will not refuse me," he said. "What is it you want, anything besides freedom? I will see that you have it. Surely there must be something. Surely we can trade."

She looked down, hesitating for a moment. "I wish to be sure my people are cared for. Beyond that, that those who raised me are safe."

"Then those will be the conditions of us forging trade alliances with Tirimia. You will have much more power here, on this throne, than you will have hiding in the forest back in your homeland. That I can promise you. You will have the ear of the king who is both good and just. You will be a princess in her rightful place. Surely that is better than hiding in a burrow like a little mouse."

She frowned, her dark eyebrows drawn tightly together, a crease forming between them. "You are fond of comparing me to animals."

"You are closer to animal than human female at the moment, sadly for me." And he was much closer to a wolf than a man. "So you will allow me to fashion you into a suitable bride. In return, I will give you what you want." There was a knock on the door to his bedchamber. "That will be the servants, ready to take you to your room."

She nodded slowly. "All right."

Some of the fire had gone out of her in the past few minutes. He found he did not like it.

That makes no sense.

No, it didn't. But nothing about the past twelve hours made any sense at all.

"We start tomorrow. Meet me in the general study after breakfast."

"What are you going to do?"

"Tame you, of course."

CHAPTER FOUR

IT TURNED OUT that Andres's definition of taming her actually meant attempting to smother her in yards of silk and tulle.

She did not feel tame in the least. Instead, she felt slightly indignant and more than a little bit irritated. Though that had been her state of being since he threw her out of his bedchamber last night.

Just thinking about it sent a hot flush over her skin, exacerbated by the cool slide of the silk that was currently being fitted to her form. She assumed the rash of heat was brought about by anger. She was angry. The way he had plucked her out of the bath, holding her against him, as though he had every right to touch her, as though she belonged to him in some way, was nothing less than enraging.

Except it didn't feel like any rage she had ever experienced before. But then, she was in a palace unlike any she'd ever been in before, wearing clothes the likes of which she had never even dreamed up before, so she imagined that was in keeping with the theme.

"Keep your shoulders straight," the seamstress said, her tone stiff, as stiff as Zara's shoulders were starting to feel.

"You heard her," Andres's voice came from beyond the screen she was standing behind. "Keep still, or it will take longer."

"I am not a child," she said, addressing both of them. "I don't need to be spoken to like one."

"Then do not fidget like one," the woman said.

Zara fought the urge to fidget just to cause trouble.

This was very strange, being the focus like this. The closest experience she had in her memory was when she had come to live at the encampment. She had been a curiosity then, but they had also been careful with her. She was a little girl who had lost her family, who was traumatized, steeped in grief.

Resources there were limited, and no one had ever procured her a new wardrobe. She'd had clothing crudely fitted to her before. Hand-me-downs that she'd acquired within the camp.

In her life before the revolution, she was certain she had experienced things like this, but there was a veil drawn over those years, memories she found difficult to access. Everything was reduced down to feelings. Still pictures in her mind. Smells, tastes.

She'd only been six when she was taken away. So much more of her life spent away from the palace than in it.

She was trying to hate it, but in truth it was difficult. The dress she was wearing at the moment was irresistible. She had never imagined she would find a dress irresistible, but she definitely had strong feelings about this one.

The bodice was fitted, soft with iridescent pink vines stitched over the silk. The skirt billowed around her like a pink cloud. And in truth, she would love to hate it for its impracticality. But it was just too pretty.

Though, even if she was having a hard time resenting the dress, she could still easily resent Andres.

"Would you like to see this one, Your Highness?" The woman spoke to Andres as though Zara weren't standing right there.

"Why not?" He sounded bored, which she found insulting. Though, had he sounded eager, she probably would have been similarly offended. He could not win with her. She had decided.

She would not allow him to. She would not marry him. She would find another way.

Though it has been said you catch more flies with honey than vinegar. And you need his help.

She ignored that thought. Yes, it was true she needed him in some capacity. But she would not be pouring out the kind of honey a man like him wanted. Andres had not been ambiguous about his intent for her. He'd told her last night that if she didn't leave he was going to…

She felt her skin growing hot again, just as the seamstress moved the screen to the side, removing the buffer that stood between herself and the rather imposing prince.

She drew in a deep breath, her breasts pushing against the tight, structured bodice. She was very conscious of the fact that his eyes were very much focused on said part of her body. He was doing it to make her uncomfortable. There was no other reason. Men did not waste time staring at her chest. Men did not waste time staring at any part of her.

Yes, she had been well protected, prior to being kidnapped and returned to the palace to be used as a political pawn, but it had not seemed to be a particular challenge for the leader of their clan to keep men away from her.

Quite the opposite, Zara felt sometimes as if she repelled people when she walked through a crowd.

The heat in his eyes was certainly not real. Which made it all the more offensive, even if it should have made it less offensive. Things with Andres simply weren't going to make sense, she had accepted that already.

"Well?" she asked, the word coming out as a command.

He put his hand on his chin as though he were considering. "You certainly look more like a princess than you did yesterday."

"I suppose it depends on your cultural point of view," she said, raising an eyebrow.

"Indeed?"

"Yes. Among my people the gold makeup is considered the mark of royalty. A mark of beauty. The robe I wore yesterday, the purple with gold thread signified that, as well. This is just a pretty dress."

"This is *couture*," the seamstress said, speaking out of turn, her tone harsh.

"Will you allow her to speak to me like that?" Zara asked.

"Yes. You were offensive," Andres said.

"My apologies," she said, not feeling particularly apologetic. It was difficult when she still felt maneuvered. Forced. Imprisoned. "I am tired." She lifted up the heavy, voluminous skirts and turned, sitting on the edge of the bed, the fabric billowing around her.

"Yes. I imagine trying on gowns all day is incredibly taxing," he said, his tone dry.

"Is it perhaps as taxing as sitting there watching someone else do it?"

"Probably not as taxing as measuring a fidgeting, surly girl." He leaned against the wall, crossing his arms over his chest, his expression laconic. "Elena," he said, addressing the seamstress, "I'm sure you could use a break. The princess and I can handle things from here."

"Yes, Your Highness." The woman was clearly unhappy with being dismissed, leaving her dresses behind for someone other than her to handle. But she obeyed.

Zara didn't think she would ever get used to that. The fact that ultimately Andres would have to be deferred to, and beyond him Kairos. She fell somewhere beneath the two of them.

It isn't as though you had any power back in the en-

campment. People put you on a pedestal, but you had no choices.

She ignored herself again, focusing instead on the growing sense of dread she felt as Elena walked out of the room, leaving her alone with Andres.

"So?" She lifted her hands, then brought them back down, gripping the fabric of the gown. "Am I suitably altered into your preferred image?"

"You have a ways to go yet," he said, his tone dry. "You still look a bit wild."

"Perhaps because I am a bit wild. Have you ever thought that no amount of work will change that? No matter how sleek you make me look, it will not change what's inside?"

"As far as I'm concerned, outward appearance is the best place to start. Changing who you are on the inside is a much more difficult task."

"Speaking from experience?"

One side of his mouth curved upward. "Experience at not managing to change it, certainly."

"If you haven't managed to change after all your years of living in this palace, what makes you think you will manage to change me and in only a couple of months?"

"I don't have to change you, not really. I only have to make it look as though you have changed. And *that*, I have ample experience with."

"I thought the ultimate goal was taming."

The other corner of his mouth turned up, and he was smiling now. Yet she didn't get the sense that there was any humor in it. "Let me ask you this. Do you think I am tame?"

She looked him over, at the perfectly tailored lines of his suit, the aristocratic cut of his features. He could have been carved, rather than made. A Greek statue with life breathed into it, rather than a man born of a woman.

He was beautiful. She found nothing feminine about the

descriptor. She would call the forest, the mountains back in Tirimia beautiful, while they were, at the same time, uncompromising and dangerous. She had a feeling Andres was both of those things in addition to being beautiful. His brother, Kairos, exuded danger, authority. With Andres it was less immediately apparent.

But she could see it. She could sense it.

Possibly that was due more to the fact that he had pulled her out of the bathtub yesterday and thrown her onto his bed, than any kind of sixth sense on her part.

Still, she was confident in her answer to his question.

"No. You aren't," she said.

"But I appear to be. Or rather, I appear to be when it suits me."

"Is that what you are suggesting I do? Behave the part of princess in public?"

"I should like for you to be a little bit more tame than you already are, as I have no interest in being bitten." Something changed in his eyes as he said the words. Anger morphing into something else entirely. To a molten heat she could swear radiated from him. Something she couldn't quite sort out. There was a lot of that between them.

"I have never bitten anyone in my life. Your concerns are unfounded."

He arched an eyebrow. "Are they?" He took a step toward her, his dark eyes boring into hers. "If I were to grab you now and throw you down on that bed, you wouldn't bite me?"

Her heart was fluttering so fast she could scarcely catch her breath. "Why would you do that?"

"Do not tell me you are so naive that you are unaware of what a man wants from a woman," he said, something hard, dangerous in his tone.

"Of course not," she said, her throat feeling tight, her face hot.

"You know what a husband wants from his wife, then," he said.

It felt as if a fire had broken out over her body, burning her in the most intimate places. She should strangle him with his own tie for daring to speak to her in such a manner. She should certainly not be overheating. "But I am not your wife."

He reached out, taking her chin between his thumb and forefinger, his hold firm, his eyes locked with hers. She should move away from him. She should kick him. She did neither.

"You will be my wife. In every sense of the word. I do like that dress," he said, his gaze roaming over her body. "I do wonder, though, if I would like it better on the floor." He leaned in closer, and her breath caught. "I wonder, if I stripped it from your body, if I were to try and claim you, would you try to bite me then?"

"Try it," she said, her voice trembling, "try it and see, you bastard."

"Dirty talk. I like it. If you think that's going to push me away, I hate to disappoint you." He moved closer then, his lips a whisper away from hers. And she found that rather than wanting to draw away, perversely she wanted to lean in closer to him. She could feel a connection forming between them, physical, real, tangible. She wanted to solidify it. She didn't want to break it. How long had it been since she felt connected to anyone? How long had it been since anyone touched her? "Sadly, for you, disappointing people is what I do best."

Then he moved away. She felt his withdrawal like a gale-force wind. Making her feel disheveled, cold.

"I resisted the urge to eviscerate you with my teeth," she said, trying to keep her tone stiff. "Perhaps I am not as uncivilized as you seem to think I am."

"Perhaps I'm not as *civilized* as you think I am."

"If you're trying to frighten me into submitting to your marriage plan, I'm afraid I must deliver the disappointing news that it will not work." She swallowed hard, calling on all her strength to form the next sentence, to meet his gaze while she spoke the words.

He laughed, a dark, humorless sound. "Silly woman. I don't need your submission. I need your cooperation."

"Is there any way I can help you without marrying you?"

"No. There isn't."

She gritted her teeth. "That's very inflexible of you."

"I am inflexible. In this instance largely because my brother is. I owe him. I disappointed him once, and I cannot do it again. This is my atonement. You are my penance."

"I suppose in that case lowering yourself onto my body will be much like crawling over broken glass."

He chuckled, which angered her because those words had cost her. Because she was dealing in subject matter she was not well versed in, trying to play that she was sophisticated. As if the things he said were unremarkable. And when she reached for a comment she thought might shock him, he didn't even have the decency to look fazed. "To the contrary, I imagine lowering myself onto your body—as you so eloquently put it—will be the most enjoyable portion of our enforced union."

"Why marriage?" she asked, feeling desperate. "Why not... I suppose I don't understand what else I could do, because I'm not entirely certain why it is you need me."

"I must marry you because Kairos gave the order for me to do so. Kairos asked me to do so to improve relations between Petras and Tirimia. Presumably there are more detailed explanations available, but he didn't give them, and I didn't ask. The reasoning was irrelevant."

"And yet you do not seem like a man who would normally feel that way. I can't imagine that you're docilely lying down and engaging in something against your will, simply because it's the right thing to do. There is some-thing else to this. There has to be."

She had no idea how she was so certain of this, only that she was. Nothing about Andres was docile. She was right, he wasn't tame. Not in the least. And yet he was al-lowing himself to be collared and muzzled by his older brother. It made no sense.

"I told you already I spent a great many years doing nothing less than exactly what I wanted. In fact, I was doing that only last week. I have made mistakes," he said, his tone uncompromising. "Mistakes I had hoped were healed by time, and circumstance that had nothing to do with conciliatory actions on my part. It turns out I was wrong."

"Be specific," she said. "Where I come from we don't deal in this kind of circular conversation. Either we tell someone what we are thinking, or we don't. There is no alluding to events and talking around the most important element of the truth."

It was true, though she was rarely included in impor-tant conversations back in her homeland. Still, the exclu-sion was not ambiguous.

"You want to know what I did? Is that it?"

"If it answers the question of why you're doing this, then yes. I feel like I have a right to know."

"So be it, then."

Andres felt strangely reluctant to tell Zara the truth. It was an oddity that she didn't know already. Everyone in his country did. Anyone abroad who read tabloids while standing in line at the grocery store knew the sordid de-tails of his past, and what had become of Kairos's first engagement.

And it was that fact that made him so reluctant to speak of it.

She didn't look at him and see the playboy prince. Didn't look at him and see the black sheep. She didn't like him, but that was based entirely on the interactions they'd had, not on any rumor or headline.

Strange that he found that refreshing, but he did.

Strange that he should care at all what she thought. But he did. He had made a practice of shedding outside opinion from an early age. When he'd first come back from the shadows and into the public eye as a teenager.

"I get the feeling you don't read a lot of gossip news."

"No," she said.

He sat down in the chair opposite her, affecting a casual posture. He was a professional at pretending not to care, particularly at moments when he cared quite a bit. "Then you won't have read about my escapades. They're legendary. There isn't a woman I can't seduce. No supermodel with sex on her mind I've ever refused. I always leave them wanting more, as I rarely stay with a woman for more than one night. I have no shame. No morals to speak of whatsoever."

He watched as the color in her cheeks rose, turning a dark pink that matched the embroidery on her dress. "Is that so?" Her voice was husky, her eyes focused somewhere on the wall behind him. He couldn't work her out. Was she simply uncomfortable in his presence, angry and biding her time, or did she feel the insistent tug of attraction just as he did?

He had been with a great many women. And while he wasn't particularly proud of that behavior when he stood back and took stock of it, it could not be denied. With his vast experience it made no sense that he would be tempted by this woman. She was not sophisticated. She was beautiful, but a great many women were beautiful. Beautiful without being too sharp, too fearsome and too wild.

She was like the wind, bottled up and stitched into a

gown. He had to wonder if she had allowed for herself to be harnessed and was simply waiting for the right moment to free herself again.

"Yes. The media always said I had no shame. I imagine that I must have some, though I have not felt any in quite some time. It's very liberating," he said, not sure why he was adding this to the conversation, "to feel no embarrassment. To feel no compunction about simply acting on your impulses because you have accepted that you are capable of nothing else. Still, I didn't imagine that I was absent of shame entirely. That isn't true of anyone except for sociopaths. And I never *thought* that I was a sociopath. Then my brother and I, and his fiancée, Francesca, flew to Monte Carlo for a bit of fun and games. Kairos, being Kairos, was having fun in a very dignified manner. Largely he was meeting with world leaders in a more casual environment. I was there to have real fun. And so, it turned out, was Francesca. While Kairos was out I threw a party in my suite. I invited every beautiful woman I could find, every man interested in engaging in a bit of gambling and debauchery. There was a lot of alcohol, as there invariably is at these things. It turns out, the right amount of alcohol is all it takes for me to lose my last vestiges of shame. It was at this party that I proved the media right."

"What did you do?" Her question, confused, mystified, enhanced by those wide dark eyes, shamed him in a way nothing else ever had. She truly couldn't guess. Couldn't even fathom the betrayal he was about to uncover for her.

Yes, if she was going to be his wife, it was best she understood now. Just who he was. Just what he was.

What your parents always knew you were.

"I screwed my brother's fiancée. I wouldn't even have remembered if it had not been for videos of the event. Not only did I humiliate my brother, but I made both Francesca and myself porn stars. That did not go over

well with her family, if you were wondering. Nor did it
go over well with mine."

Those wide eyes now registered shock, horror. He was
torn between the disappointment of watching her understand, of seeing her accept the reality of what he was, and a
strange fascination that he could still shock someone. That
she hadn't somehow sensed upon their first meeting that
he was flawed in a very real and insurmountable way. In
a way he had fully embraced. He was not a man capable
of doing things by halves. And since he could not be good,
then he had purposed to be debauched to his very core.

He had a feeling that if he tried to explain that to Zara
she would look at him as though he had grown another
head. He was struck just then at how different their lives
had been. He lived in a different world. The moment he'd
gained control of his life, he'd made it exactly what he'd
wanted. One filled with parties, as much human contact
as he wanted. A different woman every night, helping to
fill the void that might have been tempted to widen inside
him if he allowed it.

She had lived a much more solitary existence. While his
had been cluttered with noise. As much as he could possibly surround himself with.

They might as well have been from other planets entirely.

"Now," he said, not seeing the point in continuing the
discussion. "You will tell me something about yourself."

She tilted her chin up, her expression proud. "The fact
that I witnessed my family's death isn't enough information for you?"

Something uncomfortable, heavy, shifted in his chest.
"You don't want to marry me," he said.

"Of course not."

"Why not?"

"Aside from the fact that you're a stranger, you just

confessed to me that you betrayed your brother. You…
You just told me you were the most faithless man on the
planet, and now you're seriously asking me why I don't
want to marry you?"

"You said yourself you had no plans to marry. Don't
tell me now that you had fantasies of a white picket fence
and a husband who only had eyes for you. Our marriage
could be whatever you want it to be, but you haven't even
asked me what my designs on you are. You haven't asked
me what my goal is for our union, haven't given any input
on how you would like things to be conducted. You simply don't want to marry me. Which makes me think you
must have a goal apart from me."

She looked away, her jaw set, stubborn.

"Answer me, feral creature, or I will make good on my
earlier threat."

"Listen to you," she said, her head whipping around,
her lip contorted into a sneer, "the man who just professed
to being able to seduce any woman is threatening me with
his body."

"You would be seduced soon enough." He ground his
teeth together. "And I might even find I don't mind being
bitten."

"I don't wish to get my mouth dirty."

He laughed, though he felt no amusement. "I will remember that. Now, tell me. I grow impatient."

"I too am impatient, and yet no one seems concerned
about that. I have been held captive for the past two months,
before my ownership was transferred to you. Yes, I find
I am quite impatient. I've never had any say in my life. I
was born into royalty, in a position more vulnerable than
I could ever have imagined when surrounded by the stone
walls of the palace. Then I lost everyone and was taken
away to the middle of the forest. Then I was taken captive.
And now I have been delivered to you, to be your wife,

and I have no choice, yet again. Who am I? What am I to be? The pawn of whoever holds me in their hand at any given time? I must be more than that, Andres. I should like a chance to find out."

Her words touched something in him. Strange, because nothing about her should resonate. They were different. From different worlds, as he had only just been thinking. Somehow he recognized these words as though they had originated in his own head.

"You will," he said. "That is another promise I make to you. Our marriage does not have to be traditional in any sense. Not if you don't wish it. In truth, I am not suited to forsaking all others. It is simply not in me. If I have a certain measure of freedom, then you will too."

"What are you suggesting?"

"After you have our children you will be free to pursue lovers as you see fit. Or to pursue different hobbies and interests. Education if you wish."

"Interesting that you prioritize lovers over education."

"*I* would certainly choose lovers over education. But it is your choice."

She frowned. "Why?"

"Why what? Why am I offering you a choice? It does not benefit me to act as your prison guard. Neither do I have any desire to. I told you already, I don't particularly want a wife. But I owe Kairos. You understand now, clearly, I should think. All he requires is that we produce a child who can take the throne should he and his wife be unable to fulfill the task."

"I see. You only need my womb. As if that isn't an extremely large thing to ask."

"It would be a family. Blood. How long has it been since you've been a part of that?" He hated himself for using this against her. Still, he was a man with no shame, and he was hardly going to grow any on the spot.

She looked away.

"A long time," he answered for her. "Do not fight against me. Neither of us has a choice. We do not need it to be any more difficult than it already is."

He stood, getting ready to go.

"Can you call the seamstress back?"

It was not what he expected her to say. But then, he found he could not predict Zara. She didn't fall neatly into a category the way the women he often associated with did. "What do you need?"

"I'm not going to be able to get myself out of this," she said, indicating her gown.

"I am more than willing to help you with that, Princess," he said.

Heat formed a ball in his gut, a knot he could barely breathe past. Here he was, talking to her about taking other lovers once they took their vows, and yet he was getting aroused by the thought of unzipping her dress. He'd helped countless women out of couture gowns; there should be nothing exceptional about this moment. Nothing particularly interesting about this desire. And yet there was.

"No, you cannot." Her voice was stiff, her obvious distress indicating that she was not immune to him either.

"You would rather call Elena back in here just to unzip you? Seems a bit much. Do I frighten you so intensely?"

Something flared in her dark eyes. "Nothing frightens me. I already told you once. How quickly you forget."

"Then turn around."

She obeyed, and he knew it was out of sheer stubbornness more than anything else. He reached out, gripping the tab on the dress, drawing it down slowly, ignoring the slight tremble in his fingers. There was no reason for him to tremble. He was unveiling nothing more than the elegant length of her spine. Beautiful, certainly, as everything about her was, but unremarkable.

One of many naked female backs he had seen.

She looked over her shoulder, and lust hit him square and hard in the stomach. Her eyes were like no one else's.

And it didn't matter how many women he had undressed in the past, because they hadn't been her. Because it wasn't now.

Dammit, he had to get a grip.

When he had the zipper lowered all the way he took a step back, forcing his hands down at his side so he wouldn't grip the sides of the bodice and pull it down, past her hips, to pool on the floor. So that he didn't lose hold of his very tenuous control and do exactly what he had threatened to do earlier.

"Go now," she said, the words quivering.

"As you wish, Princess. But there will come a time when I don't leave once your clothes come off." He didn't know why he felt the need to add that. Didn't know why he always felt the need to get in one more hit. Perhaps because he was powerless, as was the situation in many ways. She was too. Which was perhaps why she felt the need to lash out at him.

It was why he kept striking out at her.

"Not a day sooner than necessary," she said.

"Get your sleep. Tomorrow you have yet more manners to learn."

"Will you make your best effort at getting me to bite you again?"

"No. Tomorrow I'm going to teach you to dance."

CHAPTER FIVE

FIRST, THEY HAD cut her hair. She couldn't recall the last time she'd had a haircut. For years she had allowed it to grow, hanging thick and curling past her waist, restrained most commonly by a braid. The palace stylist had taken it up to the middle of her back. It felt strange. A weight removed she hadn't been aware she'd been carrying.

After that, they had done her makeup. Entirely different from the way she had been taught to apply her own. But the woman had dusted the corners of Zara's eyes with gold powder, after rimming them in black, giving a different twist to the look Zara was accustomed to. A sort of marriage between Tirimian standards of beauty and those here in Petras.

Her gown, the third piece of her early-morning makeover, was another example of that.

Unlike the frothy confection she had worn yesterday, this gown was sleek, hugging her curves. Gold beadwork stitched onto filmy fabric that ended at her knees, turning to sheer netting past that point that was also made to glitter with the same golden details.

Her newly cut hair had been styled into glossy waves. She had never imagined her hair could look quite like this. Usually it looked much more…natural. Rough-hewn. Usually *she* looked much more rough-hewn.

She had the distinct feeling Andres would see it as a victory.

The thought would have irritated her more if she weren't so fascinated by her own reflection. Sadly she didn't have very long to linger over the stranger in the mirror. She had to go down to the ballroom because Andres was intent on teaching her to dance.

Just thinking of him made her stomach tighten, and the feeling only increased as she made her way down the stairs, down the corridor that would lead her to the ballroom. In theory. She had never been in the palace's ballroom before. She had been given rather simple directions, and since she could easily find her way through a forest, she imagined she could navigate her way through a castle.

She paused at the ornate double doors that separated the corridor from the room, and her, presumably, from Andres. This was her last moment to take a breath of air before he was standing in front of her, tightening her lungs.

She breathed in deeply, then took a step forward, grabbing hold of the handle and pulling, the heavy door giving slowly. She slipped through the open space and stopped, taking in the grand sight before her. The ceiling was high, domed, with beautiful, detailed paintings stretching over the width of the room. The walls were papered a pale blue with crushed velvet flowers, each segment of wall divided by golden molding.

She would blend in with these surroundings. A strange thought. But it was true. Now she looked as though she belonged here. Felt as though she might. She was born to this. Would have lived in it if not for the men who'd overthrown her father.

This would have been her birthright. And in reality she would very likely have been sent to marry a prince. A prince like Andres.

This could have been her fate no matter what. To be here. To be with him. Set to be his wife. Such a strange

hought. But comforting in some ways. Was this what
ier parents would have planned for her? They certainly
vouldn't have wanted her to stay in the woods for the
est of her life.

She had been… She closed her eyes for a moment,
aking a deep breath. It smelled familiar here. Of ancient
tone and wood. A palace. It reminded her of her home.
Ier first home. Of her parents and how they had cared
or her.

They had loved her. So very much. This was the sort of
ife they had wanted for her. The woman she was now, in
he dress she currently wore, was what they would have
vanted her to be.

Had she been brought up in the palace, she would be
amed already rather than being something he saw as a
eral animal.

Zara swallowed. She should not care about that. What
ie thought of her. She wasn't actually going to marry him.
'he would find a way out of this. Find a way to make it
vork for everyone.

She was not ready to be married. Least of all to a man
vho had as little choice in the matter as she did.

She had been forced into too many things. Had been
orced on too many people. Was it such a bad thing to
vish she could be chosen?

She shook off the thought, walking deeper into the
oom. It was silly to worry about things like that. Being
hosen, and wanted. Those were luxuries for people who
lidn't have to worry about survival, or about duty.

It would not have fit into either versions of her life.

Andres chose that moment to walk in the doors oppo-
ite her. She would have expected to be used to him by
iow. Would have thought that every time she saw him
he impact of his appearance would lessen. If anything,
he felt it harder, deeper, every time she saw him. He was

dressed in a tuxedo, and she could have almost laughed at the absurdity of it. Her in a ball gown, him in a suit so early in the day, in an empty ballroom. Two strangers who were being ordered to marry each other, neither of whom wanted to.

She would have laughed, but she couldn't possibly. Not when she could scarcely even take a breath. If she had felt tense at the mere thought of seeing Andres, then actually seeing him ratcheted her tension up to impossible degrees. She couldn't figure out why. Yes, he was handsome, but she had no interest in being touched by him. Being kissed by him. Or any of those other things.

She had never much minded being innocent for her age. A side effect of being kept separate from everyone else was most certainly innocence. There had been no boys to hold her hand, kiss her, during her teenage years. There had been no one to talk to her about relationships. Everything she knew she had gathered by listening and observing. And that—up until now—had been enough. Now she felt out of her depth. Confused and, worst of all, curious. Curious about what it would be like if he made good on any of his threats. Curious about what he looked like beneath those suits. Beneath that facade he wore so casually and easily she doubted most people recognized it as such. But she did. She knew what it was like to put a veneer over everything you were. To keep your manner calm, unshakable, while underneath a storm raged.

They were so very different, and yet she could see reflections of herself in his dark eyes. It made no sense. It made even less sense than her fascination with him. It should be fear. She could not deny that her feelings were certainly tinged with it, but that wasn't all of it.

Yes, it was the curiosity that disturbed her the most. If she had even a few more answers to her questions, perhaps it would not be. If she had been with a man before or at least been kissed by one, then perhaps she wouldn't be so fascinated by the shape of his mouth. Perhaps she wouldn't have so many questions about whether or not it would be as hot, firm, certain, as it looked.

He looked up, his eyes meeting hers. And he stopped. Froze, right there in the middle of the room, staring at her as though she were a foreign entity.

"You've cut your hair," he said.

She reached up, touching the silken length. "Well, *I* didn't."

"The stylist did."

"Yes." She flicked the dark curl over her shoulder. "Am I not tame?"

He tilted his head to the side. "I'm not sure. Why don't you come closer and I'll try to assess for myself?"

She found herself obeying, moving toward him warily, not quite sure why.

Perhaps it was all to do with lulling him into a false sense of security. Getting him to trust her. Yes, that was likely the reason. It had nothing to do with the tightness in her stomach, the pressure on her lungs, the dry feeling in her throat. Had nothing to do with the deadly beauty he possessed. Like a rugged landscape that beckoned you to explore, while waiting to swallow you whole.

None of that mattered. It meant nothing. It was only that fighting the entire way wouldn't help her cause, so there was no purpose in it. She had to wait and strike when it counted. So she would obey. But only for now.

It was his turn to touch her hair. He reached out slowly, and she could do nothing more than watch as he reached for her as he rubbed his thumb over the dark, silken locks. He said nothing; he only stared.

She wanted to ask if he liked it, but she realized that she shouldn't care whether he liked it or not. She didn't need him to find her beautiful; she needed him to find her sympathetic. It would probably work to her advantage if he didn't find her beautiful.

No matter how compelling he was, no matter how handsome, it didn't change what he was. He had told her in no uncertain terms. He had betrayed his brother. Not out of any real need, or great affection and love for the woman in question. Just because he could. Just because he lived to please himself. That, more than anything, should repel her. Should make his opinion on her appearance moot.

When she thought of her mother and father, of what they'd done with their positions, the changes they had died for...it should make him repellent. That he had such power and did nothing with it.

It didn't.

How disappointing to discover that she was as vulnerable to this kind of thing as any other woman.

Suddenly, he changed their positions, wrapping his arm around her waist and taking hold of her hand with his. "We're here to dance," he said. "Do you know how?"

She knew that he had asked a question, and that the question required a response, but she couldn't seem to cobble one together. He was strong. She had known that. He had plucked her out of the bathtub and carried her across the room as though she weighed nothing. Still, she had forgotten somehow. Or she hadn't fully realized. Or perhaps the memory simply couldn't do it justice.

He was strong, yes, but the true test of that was the way he held her without crushing her. Firm, but gentle. She could feel the heat of his skin radiating through the fabric of his suit, had a sense for the hard muscle beneath. So much only hinted at. Another piece of evidence to support her theory that he was hiding his real self beneath a mask.

"Put your hand on my shoulder," he said.

She obeyed again, because that was easier than trying to form words and actually figure out how to speak them. She felt every inch the creature he had accused her of being on multiple occasions. Completely ill-equipped to handle interaction with a man. As though she really had been raised by wolves and not just by a family who had a simpler lifestyle.

"You don't know how to dance," he said, answering his earlier question for her.

She shook her head, trying not to focus on the places where his hands were making contact. The way his fingers were laced through hers, the way his palm rested on her lower back. This didn't feel as if she was going along with it simply to keep him sweet. This felt like something else. It was confusing. Terrifying.

It couldn't happen.

Attraction had no place in any of this. It had no place in her life, not until she figured out what she wanted her life to look like. How could she even begin to answer that question until she got to know herself better? For some reason, standing in the center of this ballroom, held tightly in his arms, she was so acutely aware of how thin her life experiences had been until now. Every single thing was tied to her title. A title she had never been able to claim or use.

But oh, how she had suffered for it. The realization should feel…desolate. But for some reason, standing there in his arms, it was cushioned. Perhaps because someone was finally touching her. She finally felt connected. And so she asked him.

"Do you like my hair?" She couldn't bring herself to look at his face in case she caught him in a lie.

"Yes," he said, the answer slow, cautious. "Though I quite liked it before. There is something captivating about the wilder aspects you carry, I must confess."

She couldn't stop herself from looking up at him now. He was still holding her, neither of them moving. This was no way to conduct a dance lesson, and yet she found she wasn't interested in discontinuing the conversation. "What do you like about my wildness?"

"You are fierce. You fight. I can't help being compelled by that. You are everything you feel, rather than being what others should see. How can I not be intrigued by that?"

"Because you can only be what is acceptable?"

"Because I'm surrounded by people who behave themselves." It was a deflection, she was aware. He didn't deny her accusation, but he didn't admit to it either. "It is refreshing to see someone who doesn't."

"You've only seen me here. I spent a great many years behaving myself by the standards of my surroundings."

"Tell me," he said, and then he started to move. Leading her in a dance that had no music.

She held tightly to him, trying to keep from stumbling. "Tell you about my life with the clan?"

"Yes. Tell me what it meant to behave there."

"It's hard to explain. They cared for me. But I wasn't one of them." Standing in the palace, in this dress, she suddenly realized it was true. "I lived among them, but I could never say that I was accepted. Sometimes I felt as though the leader and his wife might actually… Sometimes I thought they might see me as another child…but once they had children of their own, it became very clear that wasn't the case." She'd never spoken these words out loud before. Had hardly formed them in her mind. "They were surrogate caregivers. Not a family. They observed a kind of careful distance with me, and I was expected to do the same."

"Then you didn't spend your childhood running wild?"

A smile tugged to the corner of her lips. "I did. I had all the freedom a child could wish for. I spent a lot of time wandering through the forest on my own. Talking to myself. Talking to the trees."

"Were you lonely?" he asked, and there was a strange edge to the question, a roughness that scraped against raw places inside her.

She swallowed, ignoring the discomfort inside her. "I don't know how to answer that. It was my daily life. It was normal for me. I wasn't aware of anything missing."

It was this place, this man, that made her so aware of all she hadn't had. Of the life she *should* have lived. Of the years she'd gone without being touched.

She and Andres weren't even lovers and he touched her frequently. As though it were the most casual and easy thing.

He was touching her now. Holding her close. And she was forgetting what she was here to do. Forgetting her ultimate goal. That she was only playing along now so she could use his trust later.

Right now all she could focus on was this. The way his hands felt over the flimsy fabric of the dress. The way it felt when he said she was beautiful.

The way it felt to have a man look *at* her, not through her.

What did those things matter? What did beauty matter? It had never mattered before.

She looked away from him, trying to regain control of her thoughts. "What about you?"

"I did not wander through the woods," he said.

There was something strange in his voice. She couldn't quite place what it was. More of him not saying what he was thinking. "You weren't lonely?"

"The palace is always full of people. And these days I do love a party."

Just then, looking at him, at the stark, raw emotion that flickered in his eyes for just a moment, she was struck again by that thought she'd had about being defined by her station. Except she wondered if it had been the same for him. If he was more what his title was than who he was inside. If anyone valued him at all as a man, and not as a prince.

"That doesn't matter. The camp was always crowded. There were always people. But I was never a part of them in the same way. Families, blood family, shared space. Caravans. Sometimes they would sleep altogether around the campfire. Family is the cornerstone of the clan. And I didn't have one."

"I had a family," he said, his voice rough.

"Are your parents dead too?" It was a terribly inappropriate question, one she knew she shouldn't have asked. Andres was very careful with his words. Sometimes he was direct, tactless, but that was by choice, never on accident. Other times he was careful to make a wide circle around the point, disguising it, wrapping it in something more palatable.

But she had been raised in an environment where words weren't wasted. Where honesty, honor mattered.

Still, she regretted these words.

"My father is," he said, his tone hard. "Not my mother. At least, not as far as I know."

"She isn't here." It wasn't a question.

"She hasn't been. Not for years."

"Where did she go?"

"I, my brother, my father, and all of our Secret Service don't know the answer to that. When she disappeared, she disappeared. Not, I suspect, because she was so accomplished at subterfuge, but because she did what no one expected her to do."

"What's that?"

She expected him to stop their conversation, expected him to scold her for being too bold. Instead, a faint smile tipped the corners of his mouth upward. "I think she just walked away. With nothing but the clothes she was wearing."

"Why?" Zara had imagined doing just that. But she hadn't. Because she had no money, no identification, no skills, nothing. And yet, to hear Andres say it, it was what his mother had done.

"I suspect because it was all a bit too much for her."

"Being royal?"

He stopped moving then, but he didn't release his hold on her. "Perhaps."

There was something beneath that answer, words that weren't being spoken. He frustrated her. Made her want to pound on his chest until the truth came out. But she shouldn't care. So she didn't.

"Perhaps *I* will find it all too much," she said.

He moved without warning, releasing his hold on her hand, taking hold of her chin. "You will not leave me."

She was taken aback by the sudden intensity, by the growl in his voice. "No," she said, not entirely certain she was telling the truth.

"You dance fine," he said, releasing his hold on her and stepping away from her. The chill between them was palpable, blown in on the words she had spoken, words that had carried a power she hadn't been able to guess at.

"Thank you," she said, not really meaning it. Then she doubted he had meant what he said about her dancing.

Already, she had learned something from him. Already, she was learning to hide.

"I suggest you spend the next couple of days reflecting on the best way to present yourself to the public here in Petras. There is a traditional holiday feast at the end of the week, and we will be making our debut. It will be held here at the palace, and many of the prominent citizens here in Petras will be invited, while many more will be watching on television. My brother is going to make a speech. For some reason, the populace is very interested in what he has to say."

His mask was firmly back in place. It had slipped, only for a moment, but it had.

"I don't have to say anything, do I?" The thought had occurred to her suddenly, and had horrified her. She had never had to speak in front of people in her life.

"No. In fact, it would be best if you didn't. If you can manage to stand there, look lovely and not chew on any of the chicken bones, we should be fine."

She frowned. "I'm not going to chew on chicken bones."

"I can't be sure with you."

"What sort of debut is this, exactly?"

"You will be making your first public appearance with me. As I never bring women to such things, it will be seen as significant," he said.

She opened her mouth to protest, but before she could, he turned away from her and walked out of the room, leaving her standing there in a formal ball gown, with a sinking feeling in her stomach.

CHAPTER SIX

ZARA HAD A suspicion that her gown had been selected in an attempt to soften her appearance. Pale blue raw silk with a high neckline and a formfitting shape that ended just below her knee. Her hair was pulled up into a bun, her makeup much more restrained than usual. Perhaps they thought that if she looked sedate she would be less likely to eat her lunch with her fingers.

Though in this case, appearances were certainly deceiving. She had reached the point of feeling quite desperate to escape this whole marriage bargain, stricken very much without her permission.

She was beginning to think that playing nice would get her nowhere. If Andres wouldn't take up her cause, she would carry it all on her own.

With flourish.

Her fingers were freezing. She was shaking a little bit, probably because she was cold. Snow had begun falling outside late last night, the temperatures plummeting. Petras bordered Greece, but was set deeper back into the mountains and had a climate that matched what she was accustomed to in Tirimia, more than their Mediterranean neighbor. Still, though she was used to the cold, for some reason it was getting to her at the moment.

It certainly wasn't nerves. It wasn't going to be difficult to sit at a table and eat food. She could manage that without humiliating anybody.

Whatever Andres thought, she wasn't an animal.

More people began to flood into the main doors of the palace, and Zara sank back into an alcove, her heart pounding heavily. She lifted her hands, clasping them together, holding her fingers tight in an attempt to warm them.

Okay, maybe she was nervous. She didn't know why. She had no stake in any of this. It had nothing to do with her.

She looked across the growing crowd and saw Andres's dark head, higher than the rest. Seeing him felt like grabbing a lifeline in the midst of the storm. She kept her eyes on him. He was familiar. A horizon line on a pitching sea.

He looked up, and their eyes locked. He changed course, parting the mass of people with his mere presence. She lowered her hands, still holding them together, trying to get a handle on her nerves.

"Where have you been?" he asked.

"Here. You didn't specify a meeting place."

"I didn't expect to find you hiding in a corner."

"I'm not hiding," she said, even though she had been doing just that.

"Kairos and Tabitha are on their way. We will walk in just after them. But before we go in, I have something for you."

She blinked, freezing, well aware that she looked a little bit as if she had been slapped upside the head. "For me?" Stupid, she was basically repeating his words back to him. But she had never been given a gift before, and she didn't quite know how to brace herself for it.

Her chest hurt. She didn't know why. She didn't know what to do about it.

It was a similar feeling to being alone in a caravan while everyone else sat outside around the fire. That, combined with the beautiful ache she felt when she was alone in the woods.

"Come here," he said.

He didn't wait for her to obey. Rather he wrapped his fingers around her arm and pulled her deeper into the corridor, around the staircase. Her breath caught as he reached into his jacket and brought out a small velvet box.

The ache in her chest split open, harsh, tearing pain now. And along with it, fear.

"No," she said.

"I never pretended this was anything but inevitable." He opened the box, and revealed exactly what she had feared. "You're acting like I'm presenting you with a tarantula, rather than a diamond ring."

She looked down at the beautiful, ornate ring. A platinum band with a large, square-cut gem at the center. She would have preferred a tarantula, frankly.

"You know how I feel about all of this. I don't... You didn't say that you were going to be making any official announcements today."

"I am bringing you to one of the most important events we have here at the palace. It is not an ambiguous statement on its own. The ring is implied."

"Then perhaps we should keep it implied," she said.

"No. That isn't how this works. I have made promises to you, promises that I intend to keep. Concessions have been made in order for you to feel as comfortable with this as possible. But you are not in charge. You are not conducting this show."

She found herself extending her hand, and she wasn't quite sure why. He had issued no threat, and truly, what would he do if she said no? Still, she held her hand there, steady for him, as he took the piece of jewelry from the box, and slipped it onto the fourth finger of her left hand. It felt heavy. And that heaviness carried over to her chest.

"Now it's time for us to go in."

He took the hand he had just put the ring on, curling his fingers around hers, leading her back toward the entrance to the ballroom. And she went. Because she was numb, and putting up a fight when you weren't entirely sure if your feet were still on the ground was difficult.

No. This wasn't what she wanted. She needed more time. She wasn't ready.

He said he would marry you by Christmas. By the end of the month. You only have a few weeks. What did you think?

She hadn't been thinking. She had been in denial of the fact that she had been brought here, given to Andres as though she were an object. A Christmas present for the man who had everything.

He had certainly taken possession of her as though he had every right. And he had made her feel as though perhaps they had a connection, but clearly they didn't. Or he could never force her into this. And he was forcing her. He *was*.

She was amazed at the way the crowd parted for him. No one touched either of them as they wove their way through the knot of people. They walked into the ballroom, toward the most opulent and beautifully appointed table. She recognized King Kairos immediately. You could hardly forget the man you'd been trotted out in front of as one of your country's desirable exports. Sitting next to him was a woman she hadn't seen yet. Blonde, poised, beautiful beyond measure. She was polished until she nearly glowed.

Suddenly, Zara could see why Andres thought she was feral.

In comparison to this woman, who had to be Queen Tabitha, almost anyone would appear feral. Her movements were fluid, her posture impeccable. Even her facial expressions seemed easy, smooth. She smiled at everyone with ease, looking perfectly genuine at every moment. Even when she rested, she simply looked serene. Never bored. Not tired, or upset.

Andres pulled her chair out for her, and she sat.

Tabitha turned her focus to Zara, and Zara saw for the first time the ice beneath the crystal-blue gaze. Tabitha was made of stronger stuff than she first appeared to be.

"Tabitha," Andres said, "this is my fiancée, Princess Zara. I'm not sure if Kairos filled you in. He played matchmaker."

Zara nearly choked.

Tabitha turned to look at her husband, her expression bland. "No. Kairos didn't tell me. I'm a bit surprised that he's responsible. He's not usually one for romance."

"Who said anything about romance?" Kairos asked.

Zara had no experience with these kinds of relationships. But she could recognize when people were circling each other. When they were holding back anger, spoiling for a fight. It was happening here.

Tabitha smiled, and this was the first time Zara could see how forced it was. The facade didn't hold up as well under close scrutiny.

She felt as though she was looking into her future. Shackled to a man who couldn't possibly be more bored with her existence. Pretending to be happy and serene when inside she wanted nothing more than to stand up and scream.

Manipulated by fate. Living a life beside someone who was entirely set apart from her.

The more she faced the possibility of a life without choice, the more she saw just how unhappy she'd been for a long time.

She'd been able to ignore it because there had always been a glimmer of hope for the future. A different future. One that was what she made it, rather than one she was forced into. And so she'd endured the silence. The distance. Because she'd imagined there would be something more later.

She looked again at Kairos and Tabitha, at the yawning gulf that was so clearly between these two people who sat right next to each other.

And then she picked up her fork. And dropped it back onto the plate. The clatter, loud and satisfying, startled everyone seated at the table. Zara smiled. "Sorry."

She wasn't sorry. Not in the least.

She wasn't going to go quietly. She wasn't going to accept this blandly. She had choices. And this was clearly a moment she had to seize. If Andres wouldn't listen to her, then she would use Kairos and Tabitha and their clear need for decorum above all else.

If he was only marrying for Kairos's sake, then she would make Kairos want her gone.

As long as they didn't return her to her captors, she would find her way.

She felt the hard, warm pressure of Andres's hand on her thigh and she turned to look at him. His eyes were hard. Warning.

But she wasn't so easily intimidated.

She returned his glare with one of her own, and a slow smile she knew he wouldn't believe sincere. "Is there a problem, Andres?"

"Not in the least," he said, his tone soft. Deceptively so.

Just as he didn't believe her smile, she did not believe his calm. "I'm pleased to hear that."

He squeezed her thigh. "You're quite docile."

She looked up at him again, fluttering her lashes. "I am. Quite."

"You had best remain so," he said, lowering his voice.

"Of course, my dear."